TASTE OF
TENDERLOIN

APEX PUBLICATIONS
LEXINGTON, KY

TASTE OF TENDERLOIN

GENE O'NEILL

APEX PUBLICATIONS
LEXINGTON, KY

Taste of Tenderloin

"Lost Tribe," "Bushido," and "Bruised Soul" original to this Collection; "Magic Words" first appeared in *Dark Wisdom* #10, 2007; "Balance" first appeared in Cemetery Dance #55, 2006; "Tombstones in His Eyes" first appeared in *The Grand Struggle*, 2004; "The Apotheosis of Nathan McKee" first appeared in *Unnatural Selection*, 2001; "5150" first appeared in *Horrors Beyond 2*, 2007

Apex Publications, LLC
PO Box 24323
Lexington, KY 40524

www.apexbookcompany.com
www.stevengilberts.com

First Edition, August 2009

ISBN: 978-0-9816390-0-0

Printed in the United States of America

This collection is for my friend and colleague, Brian Keene.

*He has championed my cause as a writer. This blows his public persona:
Brian Keene is a good guy, deserving of his success!*

TABLE OF CONTENTS

Acknowledgments

A special thanks to Jason Sizemore and all the staff at Apex for their complete professionalism and dedication to putting out the best book possible. Also a tip of the hat to Steve Gilbert, an artist who is able to catch the spirit of a book without giving anything away. And last I'd like to thank all the readers who buy my books, enabling me to continue pursuing my obsessions.

INTRODUCTION

I miss you. When I wanted the city, you gave it to me in blood and history. You were much, much bigger than I was. To walk your streets takes courage. To live in your belly takes a reverent respect like all good surfers have for the ocean; they know she can pound them into submission at any moment. In the veins of your alleys we are only a heart pump away from terror. In your rich heart, anything can happen. And happen fast. I've seen your young Asian armies kick a black man into unconsciousness in the middle of a busy street, busses held up to watch. I've stepped over your chalk murder outlines on the way to work, disorienting at six in the morning. I've loved your peripheral motion, your androgynous hunters, and your sad cherubs on the building faces, missing an eye, or some teeth, or both wings. I left you and your abusive pinwheel of violence and glitter...but I miss you.

I miss your juxtaposition of tenements and tourist hotels, the homeless rubbing up against the Financial District, your 60 liquor stores and swarming population of children in their little uniforms, your drugs, prostitutes, and strip clubs constantly taunting the patrons of the Theater District, your Little Saigon and abandoned banks, your methadone and public library, your transsexuals, transgenders, transvestites and museums, your bars and your bars and your bars, your dive bars and your merchant seamen that loved them, your broken wheelchairs and cable cars, your studios crammed with Asian refugees and your gay riots, your impossible parking and police bribery, your bohemians and religious rescue missions, your drug shootings and those fantastic Vietnamese sandwiches. And I love the true lies about your beautiful name; that bent tiara.

My dad doesn't drink or smoke or gamble. As far as I know, he doesn't frequent massage parlors. He's a guy who generally doesn't have a lot of patience for bullshit. And the Tenderloin has more bullshit per capita than any neighborhood in the city. So what is it about this fifteen- by seven-block radius that makes him set eight short stories inside its perimeter?

I think it has something to do with the living past of the hard-boiled 1920s that hangs around the Tenderloin, refusing to slip quietly into the annals of history. The neighborhood is still very much alive with the ghosts of the gambling dens, billiard halls, boxing gyms, and speakeasies of Dashiell Hammett, who lived at 891 Post Street--the apartment he gave to Sam Spade in The Maltese Falcon. Walking the streets of the Tenderloin, it's easy to feel Walter Tevis on your right and Nelson Algren on your left.

My father likes faces with character. He likes soulful, damaged people—at least on paper. In real life, he doesn't like anyone. Which is, perhaps, another reason why he likes the Tenderloin. It really is the most anonymous place on earth. You could bust into the corner store in a gorilla suit and pink tutu, riding a unicycle, and no one is going to look up from their shoplifting. You don't really have to engage with anyone; just bear witness to the spectacle of hard life. Also, and maybe most significantly, my father respects endurance, something the residents of the Tenderloin have in spades. You don't really understand this, what this means, until you see it for yourself. Strap your wallet to your thigh and come on down.

—Gavin O'Neill, San Francisco, 2009

LOST PATROL

*D*ense fog crashes down on the Tenderloin like a wounded cloud. *Wet, penetrating, chilling.*

On your knees, you scramble into the shelter of the cardboard tent at the dark end of the alley around the corner from Jones and O'Farrell. You hug yourself and listen intently. Nothing unusual about the night noises of the city around you, the foghorn out in San Francisco Bay a recurring mournful bellow.

Still, you're unconvinced that something hasn't followed you back here again and is lurking somewhere in the thick mist.

A trash can rattles at the end of the alley, and you hear a cat screech. A moment later, a furry blur streaks by the front of your tent.

You are unable to suppress a shudder of relief.

Carefully, you slip the recently purchased half pint of Wild Irish Rose from the pocket of your field jacket and unscrew the cap. In three long pulls, the bottle is emptied. The cheap whisky burns all the way down, bringing tears to your eyes. After a moment, you slump down on your grimy blanket, reaching inside your shirt and squeezing the medallion on the chain around your neck for comfort. In a few minutes, the medicine begins working, the warm, euphoric feeling slowly spreading out from your gut to your extremities, washing away the dread and tension.

Relaxed, you are able to slip off to sleep.

After PFC Shane McConnell had been at 3rd Platoon Base Camp on the Pokey River for a little over four months, he made his first real patrol mission with Second Squad. He'd been out a half dozen times the past month and a half on day-long search and destroy sweeps this side of the river, but there were never any NVA units or VC in the surrounding area east and north along the river. It had been kind of like Advanced Infantry Training Regiment back in the states at Camp Pendleton. The S & D training had been just about as mind-numbingly dull.

But this present patrol was the real deal; it was why they were stationed there.

They had first picked up supplies at the airfield. Then, loaded down like Himalayan sherpas, they had crossed the river on a bobbing pontoon bridge near the tiny village of Duck Soup. From there they had humped along a steep, winding trail on the other side, and soon disappeared from airfield view into the thick jungle. Second Squad's primary mission was to hump various supplies and ammunition to a special operations unit across the river. The unit contained a never-specified number of detached 3rd Force Recon personnel who reportedly lived with and led three or four clans of fierce Hmong tribesmen, marauding from a secluded sanctuary high up in the jungle-covered mountains.

They met at pre-arranged drop sites, the location and route changing with each patrol. The longest ones kept them out three nights, but each at least required an overnighter. Half the squad carried extra small arms ammunition, medical supplies, and grenades in their backpacks; the other half packed 60mm mortar rounds wrapped in old used socks with the bore-riding arming pins safely double-taped down.

At their first break, Shane plopped down next to a guy named Ward, a college dropout who everyone called Psycho because of his rambling, emotional, complicated, and often bizarre beliefs and theories about almost everything. Shane felt the guy's convoluted intellectual opinions sometimes had a kind of compelling relevance to the craziness of everyday life in the Crotch, as the grunts called the corps. It was from Psycho that Shane had first heard the DOD-sanctioned explanation for why U.S. forces were even being deployed in Vietnam: the so-called Domino Theory, indicating that if South Vietnam fell to the communists, other countries of Southeast Asia would soon topple, too. Psycho thought it a visually dramatic but "damned flawed theory," not well supported by the socio-political or historical background of the region. "No way, man," he explained. "Thailand, known as Siam for most of its history, has been an independent kingdom for over a thousand years. Most of Burma was independent and unoccupied for just as long." He talked a lot about U.S. forces really being in Vietnam to protect long-term colonial interests established by the French across Indochina, a complicated and rambling geo-political argument that he apparently supported, although Shane was never positive about that.

"Hey, man," Shane asked Psycho after catching his breath, "how come they don't just fly this shit in by 'copters?" They were both resting on their packs, cams damp with sweat. "Seems better, more efficient, than using us ground-pounders. And for sure much easier on our frigging backs."

Psycho grinned cynically. "Yeah, you got that right, Mac. But Captain Van Zant says that there isn't enough good level and cleared ground for a drop zone where we're headed up in the mountains. Which is complete bullshit. It doesn't take much to clear away growth for a small 'copter pad. But I think the real reason is that we cross too far west, beyond where we're actually supposed to be, you know." He added in a much lower voice, "Brass doesn't want any choppers over there dropping supplies to Force Recon advisors who aren't even over there. You get my drift?"

"You think we're actually crossing over the border of 'nam?" Shane asked, unable to mask his doubt.

Psycho shrugged, then nodded. "Yeah, I definitely do. We've got to be slipping into Laos, maybe sometimes even the northern tip of Cambodia, when we hump just a couple of days farther south from here." He paused, studying Shane's skeptical scowl. "What? You never looked at any of those maps pinned up in headquarters? Checked the scale? Got curious about the estimated location of our drop points?"

Shane thought about that for a moment. Before this patrol, he hadn't really been too interested in reading maps or visualizing scale, drop points, and such. But he conjured up the image of the big map with their approximate base camp location on the river, the actual short distance—as a bird flew—to the border, and the current mission's drop point. *Jesus Christ!* He realized it might be true. Psycho could be right. They were most likely headed across the border into Laos.

"Then who are Force Recon hitting with this shit?" he asked, tapping his pack. "They must be doing more than just training. Are there North Vietnamese Army over there in Laos and Cambodia? Or maybe Viet Cong? Or what?"

"Who knows, man?" Psycho said, shrugging again. "Must be someone there to shoot at. They're using up a hell of a lot of ammo and grenades for something, or maybe just stockpiling a shitpot of stuff for something else that's coming down the line." He paused again for a moment, then added with a grim expression, "But I'm not so sure the guys we're supplying are even Third Force Recon advisors, man. They never have any Hmong tribesmen with them on the drop pickups, and—"

"Who are they, then?" Shane cut in.

"You just wait and see for yourself," Psycho answered in a conspiratorial whisper. "Hell, I'm not so sure these dudes are even *alive*. I think they might be elements from that scary-ass Lost Patrol bunch. You heard 'bout them?"

Shane nodded and sat up, frowning. He took a long draw from his canteen, not sure Psycho wasn't trying to pull his leg, take advantage of the gullible new guy. Of course he'd heard of the legendary Lost Patrol. It was one of the major Vietnam myths. Supposedly, they were ghostly, zombie-like remnants of a USMC infantry platoon ambushed somewhere farther north. Stories said they roamed the deep jungle in tattered, rotting camouflage, striking fear into the hearts and minds of friend and foe. There was scuttlebutt of the raggedy ghosts everywhere across South Vietnam, distant sightings often on the same day. Maybe there was more than one patrol. Some private on mess duty from Third Squad had told Shane that it was true, the dings really did believe the ghostly scuttlebutt and were scared shitless of the Lost Patrol. Charlie prisoners often swore to actual sightings and hostile contact.

But there? At their drop zone? So far south up in the mountains? Shane shook his head. Man, that was some kind of spooky, crazy shit to even remotely consider.

Growing up, he had never believed in ghosts or any other supernatural stuff, but he had never thought too much about it, really—not until coming to 'nam. Now he wasn't so sure. Everyone was blatantly superstitious. Half the platoon wore St. Christopher medals, even though only a few were actually Catholic. Others carried rabbits' feet, lucky coins, or different kinds of Asian good fortune charms, including magical tattoos they brought back from R and R in Bangkok or Hong Kong. There were more tics and odd ritualistic behaviors happening before going on a patrol than on a baseball team coming up to bat in the bigs—a few guys even wore their same "lucky" shorts, socks, or whatever, regardless of whether they were clean or not. Shane grinned sheepishly because he'd recently bought the famed Tibetan Buddhist chant from a Navy corpsman returning home—*om mani padme hum*—etched in elegant Sanskrit on a tiny silver medallion he wore around his neck. He figured the good luck mantra couldn't hurt. But the Lost Patrol, so far out? That was just too squirrelly. Still, he couldn't keep himself from shuddering slightly.

"Saddle up," Sergeant Owens ordered, coming down the line of resting grunts.

Reluctantly, the squad slipped back into their heavy packs, picked up their weapons, and began climbing the narrow trails again. Up, always uphill; the muggy heat trapped under the low-hanging jungle canopy seemed not to cool down even a degree after they had climbed hundreds of feet higher in elevation. Soon, their cams were soaked, and everyone was huffing and puffing and dying of thirst.

Late that afternoon they made camp and immediately set up a defensive perimeter, a tight circle of seven two-man posts—half on guard, half supposedly sleeping. Big O and the Navy corpsman assigned to the patrol shared a position.

No one really slept, of course. Shane was lucky to even doze off for a few minutes. It had rained heavily a day before the patrol's mission, and the dense forest overhang was like a grand drip system, creating a kind of clinging, thick mist that hovered near ground level around dusk. The jungle grew dark early, and despite what he might have believed back home about tropical forests being quiet at night, there was a teeth-jarring cacophony of strange sounds: coughing growls, deep-throated howling, sharp barking, high-pitched squeaks, deep croaking and chirruping. Beneath that, in the distance, just at the threshold of hearing, lay a humanlike whispering, the words indistinct, foreign. The latter sound was perhaps only imagined, a kind of group paranoid delusion. Over it all sounded the very real and steady resonating hum of thousands of insects, making the hair on Shane's neck prickle as if it were the dry, irritating sound of a piece of chalk scratching against a blackboard. He knew in his heart that every one of those fucking bugs would visit him personally sometime during the night, each heavily armed with a probe, sting, bite, poke, or scratch, some highly venomous and others perhaps bearing some horrible exotic disease. His helmet net provided no defense against being bit or stung on the hands, wrists, ankles, or any other briefly exposed skin. Shane tried to rest, keeping everything covered up as best he could, but he was only able to lie there dozing, listening and scratching frantically.

The risks and dangers of meeting an enemy patrol were real enough to Shane, but he pushed them to the back of his mind. The creepy-crawly hazards, lurking right near them in the tropical forest, were more immediate and attacked relentlessly throughout the early night. And they were *noisy*. Tex, his fire team leader and perimeter post partner, had explained to Shane the first night out in the deep jungle that the din was a preferable state, really their best friend. If the jungle went suddenly quiet, that was the time to worry—abrupt silence tightened up every experienced grunt's sphincter muscle in a hurry. It meant something unusual was happening out there, just beyond their view, something—or perhaps someone—dangerous moving about quietly in the darkness with evil intentions.

The next morning they ate cold K-rations, no fires.

The heavily laden squad struggled along through the thick upland forest, finally reaching the coordinates of the meeting point in the early evening. No one was there to meet them. Not yet.

They made camp and waited.

At dusk, the jungle came alive again with its grinding cacophony of sound. Second Squad ate another cold meal and waited, nerves tight and exposed. The only relief was when Big O moved among them, joking and cheering them up individually.

At about six, the jungle suddenly turned quiet.

Dead silence.

Not even one pesky mosquito ventured forth to harass Shane or any of his buddies.

He, like most of the squad, looked about wide-eyed, his

throat tight and his stomach muscles clenched painfully. He sweated heavily, a clammy, itching dampness accumulating in his crotch and underarms, laden with the sour smell of fear.

Quiet…except for the sound of operating handles on individual M-16s sliding ominously back and forth into place. Rounds were chambered as everyone hunkered down into a prone firing position and waited anxiously for something to happen.

Time crawled by slowly.

6:01, 6:02, 6:05, 6:10…6:30.

The fog settled in, clinging to the nearby tree limbs and vines like white gauze, adding to the eerie mystique of the darkened, silent jungle.

Big O crawled up and down his line of exhausted, nervous ground-pounders, patting shoulders, whispering encouragement, handing out sticks of Doublemint and advising everyone to "Try to hang loose."

Impossible.

Shane tried a trick he'd learned back at AITR to increase hearing acuity. He pinched his nostrils together with a thumb and forefinger, then blew hard, making his ear canals pop. He swallowed dryly, cocked his head to the side, and listened intently.

Still not a sound out in the muggy night.

So it was shocking when, a few minutes later, the strange face first appeared in the mist.

The pale, thin, almost skull-like shaven head stared at them with its sunken dark eyes like an apparition in the fog. No more than ten feet away, it was a still, macabre white portrait framed against a dark, foggy background.

A body coalesced from misty particles, wearing Marine cams, with arms extending an M-16 in a neutral position overhead. Finally, the whole man stepped cautiously forward into better view.

Shane swallowed, his throat dry and scratchy.

The gaunt man's uniform was washed out and tattered, though not quite rotting off him. It no longer bore rank, name patch, or insignia of any kind—just a faded, colorless set of Marine cams. He approached Big O in a silent, unnatural movement—almost catlike. They spoke only a few words, then the strange Marine made a slow lifting signal with one arm.

Only a few feet away from where Second Squad lay hunkered down—so close they could have reached out and touched the Marine—five sunken-eyed demons popped up out of the waist-high grass. Not demons, really, but gaunt, pale men wearing torn, faded shirts and pants that barely resembled uniforms. They all carried M-16s slung carelessly over their shoulders.

How long have they been that close? Shane asked himself, trying again with little luck to work up a bit of moisture into his mouth.

"Turn over to the men in front of you what you're carrying in your backpacks," Sergeant Owens ordered hoarsely.

The grunts obeyed immediately, relieved to be finally rid of their heavy burdens. After taking the supplies from Second Squad, the pale-faced phantoms gracefully slipped away, despite their bulging packs, and disappeared silently back into the dark jungle. Soon, their bald, gaunt leader—whomever the fuck he was—followed. A sickeningly sweet stench hung in the damp air, even after they'd disappeared.

"They weren't any Lost Patrol, no way," Shane murmured to himself under his breath, but he felt no real conviction. The comfort was shallow, like whistling while passing a graveyard at night.

On the way back out of the mountains, the jumpy patrol bunched up too tightly on a narrow, steep trail. Every man froze as one when they heard the first metallic *plunk*—the characteristic echoing sound of a mortar round being dropped into a firing tube.

Plunk...

Before the second echo finished, the experienced members of the squad had hit the ground and were digging in, jacking rounds into chambers and preparing to return fire.

Shane remained standing in place, even after the third *plunk* died away, finishing the unseen enemies' first triangulation of mortar fire. Charlie was trying to zero in on them.

Tex finally managed to pull Shane to the ground, a moment before the wet floor all around them began to explode, mud and jungle debris raining down on the whole bunched-up squad.

Ear-shattering chaos broke loose on the patrol—more mortar rounds plunking and booming, accompanied by small arms fire chattering away and the pinging of grenades being armed. The latter arced through the air and exploded with sizzling streams of white phosphorus, audible even over the rhythmic *tat-tat-tat* of heavy machine guns.

Dumbstruck and disoriented, Shane's consciousness registered none of these dangerous sounds. He didn't even try to return fire. Instead, he clutched his helmet and curled into a fetal ball in the jungle mud. The cries, moaning, death rattles, and airborne body parts made only a passing impression on his conscious mind. Moments later, with his heart thumping wildly, Shane felt a sharp burning sensation along his neck, below his ear. His right shoulder simultaneously went numb, and then a feeling like being drowned overwhelmed what was left of his dulled sensibilities.

Blackness.

Days later, PFC Shane McConnell regained a drug-addled consciousness in a receiving hospital back in California at Travis AFB. The deep shrapnel wounds in his neck, shoulder, and back were operated on before he was eventually transferred to the VA hospital in the North Bay at Martinez. They did an excellent job on his physical wounds, but not so well on his head. He experienced horrible recurring flashback nightmares, images of disembodied bloody heads, arms, and legs swirling about in the air around him in the jungle. The meds and talking to doctors did nothing at all for his permanently damaged soul.

Medically discharged from the USMC with a small monthly disability check, Shane soon found himself living in San Francisco's Tenderloin, mostly involved in a 24/7 drinking contest with himself. When his funds ran out each month he panhandled, but could never make ends meet. Finally, he became homeless, unable to support his escalating alcohol and drug habits and the residential hotel rent. Life on the street was tough, and during the wet winter following his discharge, he went back and forth three times to Martinez, diagnosed each time with recurring bouts of pneumonia. The final time, the doctors warned him of the high risk of his self-destructive lifestyle.

Shane ignored them and returned to the 'loin's shuffling Legion of the Forgotten and Never Remembered.

The sudden silence startles you awake. Sweaty and gasping for breath, you sit up, your hand tightly clutching the silver medallion hanging from your neck. Something is wrong. A sickly sweet stench assaults your nostrils, making them itch. With an effort of will, you stand and force yourself to step outside the tent.

Heavy fog is trapped under the canopy, the jungle absolutely quiet.

You wait and watch, resigned, knowing they are there, just out of view.

Finally, figures begin to coalesce in the mist…ghostly figures, faces pale, eyes sunken, their clothes torn and tattered—

You recoil with surprise.

Because you recognize the closest figure, despite his gaunt features and deeply sunken eyes.

It's Sergeant Owens.

And right behind him, in the mist at the jungle's edge, appears Tex… and then

Psycho, and all the others from Second Squad.

Big O points at you and gestures with his thumb over his shoulder.

For a moment, you hesitate.

Then you bend down and pick up your backpack, sling your M-16.

It's time to mount out.

MAGIC WORDS

"We conjure miracles for our clients.
Show me the magic, people."
—Thomas Brookings, Double B & A

The old, dark-skinned woman sat in the lotus position alone in her cardboard tent, staring out into the night as the fog crept into the alley from the bay, visualizing the young man's distinctive features, his hair and his left eyebrow. Eventually, she nodded; he was the one, of course. She opened the black book and again traced the procedure outlined in the ancient text, patiently mouthing the words from a language even older than her native Romany. It would take careful execution and time to complete. Smiling wryly, she sucked in a deep breath. She had been hunting a long time to find this young man—several more months, or even years, to complete the task meant little.

The Great American Music Hall in San Francisco was located on O'Farrell Street, on the fringe of the Tenderloin near the infamous Mitchell Brothers strip joint. At five thousand square feet, the concert hall wasn't really large enough for modern concerts like the Warfield on Market Street or Shoreline down the peninsula or Concord Pavilion over in the East Bay. No, the hall usually featured top local music talent or personalities with cult followings doing spoken word, like Jim Carroll and Henry Rollins, or occasionally a relatively unknown musician, singer, or personality just about ready to break out nationally. Like tonight with Daz L, the Jamaican reggae-hip hop artist, who had packed the place with a standing-room-only crowd.

At a little after 10:45, the fans—mostly hip, young, and casually dressed—exited the venue laughing and talking loudly, heading for nearby parking lots or the clubs up along Van Ness. Two older white guys, dressed deceptively like lawyers, stood out as they watched the departing crowd from the curb in front of the hall. Lucas Somerville, tall and broad-shouldered in his Italian suit, had a small, distinctive splash of silver in the short-clipped black hair just above his left eyebrow; the eyebrow itself was cleaved in half by a pencil-thin silver line. Only the deep, dark circles under his eyes and slightly drawn expression marred his distinguished, athletic appearance, suggesting an unsettled mental state. His bespectacled and bald older colleague and mentor, Hubie Jensen, was dressed a bit more conservatively in a dark blue English worsted suit.

After carefully assessing the departing crowd, Jensen spoke, his normally calm, precise voice pitched higher than normal. "The crowd loved Daz L, Luke. Just look at their excitement. And did you notice Santana and his friends slip in up front just before the first number? Yes, this young man is going to definitely be a huge star...perhaps even bigger than Bob Marley."

Jensen should know. He'd been an aficionado of authentic reggae music in the late '60s and '70s and had written several articles on the music and Rastafarian movement for Rolling Stone. In fact, he had seen Marley and the Wailers when they had come to San Francisco for their only local performance just before the star's premature death, and Jensen had reviewed that concert for San Francisco Magazine.

"Tom Brookings is amazingly perceptive, almost clairvoyant," Jensen added, referring to the legendary senior partner of Double B & A., as the Brookings, Brown, and Associates advertising firm was known down in the financial district.

Luke nodded his agreement. Even though he cared little for hip hop and knew nothing about reggae music, he found the young Jamaican's charismatic performance truly impressive. Daz L's first CD, "Trenchtown Man," was already climbing the charts in London. He didn't doubt it would do the same in the states. They had just watched an emerging star.

"Yes, if handled correctly, this young man is going to be a starred account," Jensen said, "And it all starts with your little cologne promotion. You better pull out all the stops on this one—magazines, billboards, TV, radio spots, movie ads, and the whole promotional package. Who knows where this will lead?" The older man nudged Luke's shoulder playfully. "I suspect this will make them all forget Asian Dawn. I bet you are already working on a product name, some good ideas."

It wasn't true. Luke was completely devoid of ideas, didn't have a clue yet. He'd been procrastinating since being assigned the account a week prior. But he nodded anyhow, forcing a confident grin he didn't really feel. Asian Dawn was the Hong Kong frozen fast food account he'd let slip away early last year to a NYC competitor—a potential starred account, too. It had started his slump. And of course he picked up on Jensen's subtle warning: as the Daz L account senior executive, he'd better not fuck this one up. A big meeting with the singer's management people was set for Friday afternoon; three days away and clock ticking. They wanted a major campaign, timed to take advantage of Daz L's upcoming national concert tour, to promote a scent already being produced by a little Jamaican firm, West Kingston Herbals, Ltd. Something they had made special for Daz L and sold on the island, but a product Luke's people thought had real commercial possibilities in the states. Oh, yeah, Luke understood what was at stake. This would be his *last* chance at Double B & A.

"Want to stop at the Shady Lady for a drink?" Jensen asked.

Luke checked his watch and shook his head. "I have to go with Lauren to one of her twelve-step meetings."

He had no intention of making that midnight meeting after Lauren finished her four to twelve shift at UCSF Hospital in an hour or so. He needed to make an unaccompanied pit stop down the street at the Corner Mart to see his man, George. Even with the problems at work, juggling finances, and coping with Lauren, Luke had recently managed to cut back on the booze and especially the blow. Neither was really a problem for him, not like Lauren's ongoing struggle. No, he could take it or leave it. Sure, he occasionally accompanied her to one of the meetings, but just to keep peace. Man, she could be a ball-busting nag. But tonight he needed a little pickup, a mental edge. He had some serious thinking to do. First, he needed a booty-whipper brand name for the scent, something readily identifiable with Daz L and his Rastaman image, then some kind of catchy line or two, something to key a national advertising campaign. All before Friday.

"Okay, give my best to Lauren," Jensen said kindly, patting Luke's shoulder. "You have a big opportunity here, Luke. I'll check in sometime tomorrow afternoon, see how you're coming along. Okay?"

"Sure thing, Hubie. See you then," he replied, watching the

older man cross the street to his BMW. Then Luke pulled out his cell and punched in Lauren's number.

"Hey, babe," he said when she answered. "Can't make your meeting. Hubie and I have some stuff to kick around about this guy Daz L. Looks like it might be a big account. Good opportunity for me."

"Okay, I understand," she answered, the disappointment obvious in her tone. "You guys aren't going to a bar?"

"Of course not," he said, frowning and vigorously shaking his head. "I'm on the wagon just like you. We're just grabbing a cup of coffee."

"That's fine," she said. "Thanks for the call, sweetie."

"See you later, babe," Luke said. He punched off, sighed under his breath, and slipped the cell phone back onto his belt, mentally smothering the slight twinge of guilt.

Luke decided to walk the three or four blocks, even though the Tenderloin at night creeped him out. The 'loin was without a doubt the armpit of the city. Because of the full moon, he knew that every panhandler, homeless person, hooker, junkie, and crazy would be hyped up and crowding the street, but he couldn't drive. His new black PT Cruiser convertible would draw too much attention sitting in front of the Corner Mart while he scored some coke. He'd have to walk down O'Farrell, do his business, and then hike back up to his car.

As he expected, the 'loin was really loud that night: the gaudy neon crackled, loud music blared out of the bars, people screamed down from second and third story windows, cars braked and honked, and sirens wailed like wounded animals. Luke negotiated the crowded sidewalk, avoiding eye contact with the general riff raff—until the redheaded black hooker blocked his way.

"Hey man, ya'll looking to party?"

He glanced up into her heavily painted face and shook his head dumbly. Even several feet away, her smell was overwhelming. Heavy, cheap perfume did not quite conceal her musky she-scent, and there was a hint of something else…the unwashed jockstrap/sweat sock smell of a high school locker room. He almost gagged as he slipped away from her.

"Hey, sissy boy, fuck you; the Castro is back that way."

Moving quickly deeper into the Tenderloin, Luke passed more of society's discards—hustlers ("Hey, man, ya lookin'?"), panhandlers ("Yo, pal, gimme a buck for coffee"), junkies, crazies talking to parking meters, and wave after wave of scruffy, smelly street people.

That was what he ultimately hated about the Tenderloin; the *smells* nauseated him. The heavy scent of curry, suddenly wafting down from an open apartment window; the sweet-tangy smell of something organic rotting in the gutter; even the double Muni buses seemed more offensive in the 'loin, belching out great polluting clouds of black diesel fumes. The foul odors seemed to cling at street level, held in by the ever-present fog, pervading his clothes like cigarette smoke. He made a mental note to drop his suit off at the dry cleaners the next day on the way to work.

Half a block from the Corner Mart he winced, swung out toward the curb, and bypassed a derelict collapsed in a doorway among the accumulated debris of the night. *Jesus Christ*, he swore silently, pinching his nostrils and restraining himself from actually kicking the bum in the head. Above all, Luke Somerville detested the acrid smell of the homeless: the stink of failure.

Thankfully, he managed to make the doorway of the Corner Mart without another confrontation of any kind, only to find a stranger behind the cash register.

"Where's George?" Luke demanded as if the missing older clerk were AWOL.

"I am sorry, sir, he is not here tonight," the young man said in proper but accented English. He was probably from the same ethnic background as George. East Indian or perhaps Pakistani. Luke wasn't sure. It didn't matter. What did matter was his regular coke contact was missing. The realization jangled his already tightly strung nerves.

"Do you expect him back sometime this evening?"

"No, he is attending a family celebration."

"Well, is there a number I can reach him at?"

The clerk shook his head. "Sorry, sir."

Damn, I need some blow tonight, Luke almost screamed back at the guy, just barely able to restrain his sense of growing panic.

"Perhaps I can help you with something," the young man suggested.

Luke thought fast. "Well, you see, George usually helps me, ah, with takeout, you know? Maybe you could take care of it for me?"

The young man nodded, eyeing Luke carefully. "I see. By any chance do you have a card, George's card?"

A card? Oh, yeah, George had given him a business card several months ago. Luke dug his wallet out of his pocket and searched through it, his hands shaking. Finally, he located the card, and with a sigh of relief, he placed it on the counter by the cash register.

CORNER MART

O'Farrell & Hyde

Groceries/Liquor/Take Out Deli

The young guy turned it over, then smiled. On the back of the business card, George had carefully inscribed in upper case block letters:

O.K.

GEORGE Z.

The clerk looked up from the card and nodded. "How much takeout did you need tonight, sir?"

Luke slid a hundred-dollar bill across the counter.

After pocketing the money, the young man left the cash register and disappeared into the back of the little store. He returned in a moment with a small brown paper bag. He placed this in front of Luke, who glanced into it. Inside was a plastic baggie containing a small amount of coke.

"Thanks, man," Luke said over his shoulder as he quickly departed the store. He paused in the brightly lit entry, glancing up and down O'Farrell. Seeing no one who looked suspiciously out of place, he turned left to head back up toward Van Ness.

A hand gripped his arm, stopping him in his tracks. Luke gasped, his heart leaping into his throat.

But it was only a bag lady. An old woman who was vaguely familiar. Yes, he was sure he'd seen her before. Several times in the Tenderloin, over in the financial district, maybe once out in the marina. He remembered her, not because of her exceptionally disheveled appearance, but because of a special aspect of her attire. She had the normal layered appearance of the homeless— grimy garment piled on filthy garment—but over it all, across her shoulders, she wore an indigo scarf, not nearly as greasy and frayed as the rest of her clothes, decorated with beautiful gold arabesque markings around its border. It made her stand out from the usual grey and brown derelicts pushing shopping carts. Up close, he noticed that her eyes were unusual, too: one a faded denim, the other a rich mahogany.

"Wait, mister, I can help you." The strange woman interrupted his reverie in an accented, gravelly voice. She appeared to be African, or Arab, or perhaps Spanish.

Luke pulled his arm away from the bag woman. How could this derelict possibly help him in any way? As if privy to his thoughts, the woman peered into his eyes and said, "I can help you with something you need most deeply at the moment."

He hesitated.

She nodded. "It is true, I have the words."

What did she mean? *What fucking words?* Despite being intrigued by the woman's enigmatic language, it was getting late and he needed some time to do a line or two and give some thought to the men's scent promotion before Lauren got home. He turned away to head uptown, back to his car.

"The new account...your last chance."

Surprised, he turned back to face the woman's almost mesmerizing gaze.

"What do you mean?"

The strange old lady did not have the normal rank odor of her kind. She had no noticeable smell at all.

"I will write something that will benefit you and the new account," she said, "but in return you will need to write something for me."

Luke froze in place. Of course she was delusional. How did

she even know about the Daz L account, his slump, or, for that matter, what he did for a living? Who the fuck was she? He wasn't sure of any of the answers, but he was sure of one thing: spotting the old lady around in the past hadn't been random. The woman had obviously been stalking him. Now that he thought about it, he realized that maybe he'd first seen her the same day as the disappointing loss of the Asian Dawn account, the day his run of bad luck had started. Yes, he was sure of it. Jesus. He needed to get away from her. In addition to bad luck, she might be dangerous.

But when Luke tried to move, he discovered her gaze held him spellbound. He couldn't move any of his limbs. It was almost as if she had somehow lassoed him with an invisible rope.

"Okay," he finally whispered, "tell me your words."

"I need to write them for you in a special spot. Where words alter the future. Come this way." She half-turned, breaking eye contact and gesturing toward the entry to a nearby darkened alley.

Oh, no. Not back in there. Not this kid.

Luke's pulse was racing, alarms going off in his head. He could move on his own again, and knew he should turn away. Run. Escape. But he was enthralled by her voice and the cryptic sentence about the future; instead of paying attention to instinct, he felt compelled to follow the woman into the shadowy alley, expecting to be hit over the head at any moment. Or stabbed. Or shot. Or something else terrible. On shaky legs, he closely accompanied the old woman to the very back of the smelly, dead-end alley, to a brick wall.

A streetlight from back on O'Farrell flickered to life as if on cue and cut across the darkness of the alley, dimly lighting up the wall. It was an amazing collage of colorful graffiti: cartoon characters, tagger names, polemic political expressions, crude pornographic art, several catchy sexual expressions—JOSE SUCKS THE BIG JUAN and DERON'S MOMMA STOOP FOR THE GROUP—and a blank spot. Right in the middle of the kaleidoscope of graffiti was an empty rectangular box, its perimeter denoted by a thin indigo border and gold symbols marked in a pattern similar to the woman's scarf. For a moment, peering into the box, Luke had the sensation of falling, of being sucked into deep space. He almost expected to see stars, galaxies, and nebulae rushing by.

He blinked. *Whoa, get a grip, man!*

"Here, I will write," the bag lady announced, moving up to the mysterious box. She took out a common fine-tipped indigo felt pen, popped off the top, then turned back to him before she began to inscribe anything. "I write something for you. But you must return *when* I call and write something for me in this same box. It may not be for a month or two, even years. But you must immediately come when I summon you and write. Do you understand, Lucas Somerville?"

Jesus, she even knew his name. He nodded and cleared his throat. "Yes, I understand," Luke said, unable to suppress the anxious curiosity in his tone.

The woman turned and very carefully printed out two lines:

RAZ L DAZ L

For the discriminating gentleman.

Luke stared raptly at the block for several moments.

Of course this was it. He grinned inwardly. Just what he needed for the Friday meeting at Double B & A. Incorporating Daz L's name into the brand name of the scent; the name's memorable, the over-the-top-garishness seeming to clash with the line suggesting refined good taste, but actually fitting together perfectly. It resembled so much of his best work, based on the contrasting of images and words. Luke loved what the bag lady had written. Magic words. He looked into her mismatched, strange eyes again and nodded his approval.

"Okay, Lucas Somerville, I will see you again here at this same hour sometime in the future." She made the pronouncement like a judge, her voice colder than the bay fog that had slipped into the alley around them. "Do not make me track you down."

"I will be here at this same time whenever you call," Luke said, glancing at his wristwatch: 11:35 p.m., March seventeenth.

The woman slipped past him, heading back out toward O'Farrell.

Luke remained in place for a few seconds, wondering what

had just happened. The rectangle with the funny symbols around it was blank, deep space again. He didn't believe in crazy-ass stuff like magic. Still, he couldn't hold back a shudder as he followed the strange old woman's footsteps back out to O'Farrell Street.

After the enthusiastic Friday meeting at Double B & A, significant events unfolded quickly. During the national tour, Daz L became an overnight super-star, and almost immediately thereafter the cologne brand name and expression appeared on billboards across the country, right after debuting in every national magazine from *Oprah* to *Sports Illustrated*. Within six months, Raz L Daz L was the most popular men's fragrance in the U.S. The expression "Raz L Daz L for the discriminating gentleman" became as lauded in advertising promotional circles as "Where's the beef?" West Kingston Herbals, Ltd. became the largest employer in Trenchtown and soon in all of Kingston, eventually negotiating to have Raz L Daz L produced in two additional plants in Oakland and London to meet the escalating world demand. A TV ad, conceived and directed by Luke, appeared with Daz L standing between two gorgeous, skimpily dressed models, grinning and declaring in his thick Jamaican voice, "Hey, mon, Raz L Daz L da ladies."

Soon after beginning the initial promotion for Raz L Daz L, Luke was putting in fourteen-hour days, often attending meetings in several different time zones and countries in the same day. In addition to the cologne, he promoted half a dozen other products, even a Saturday morning TV cartoon with the voice of Daz L. At the end of nine months, the singer's account at Double B & A was making money faster than the old U.S. Mint down on Fifth Street printing a new run of dollar bills.

As the too-short days flew by and demands on his time increased, so did Luke's gauntness and the deep bags under his eyes. He'd even developed a permanent slight tremor in his hands. His appearance caused his friend Hubie Jensen to press him about his health.

"Hubie, everything is fine. Busy and hectic, but just fine. Okay?"

"And Lauren?"

"Well, that isn't working out; Lauren's still coping with her substance abuse problem, you know?" That was a damn lie. Lauren was doing well in her recovery. He told himself that she left him because she just had too much competition. He had succumbed to his own hype and was using Raz L Daz L. The TV ad implication was indeed prophetic: the ladies loved it. But deep down he knew that his womanizing wasn't the reason Lauren had moved out. She'd gone soon after he'd brought up the subject of breast enhancement. In a teary voice she had insisted that he cared deeply about only two things: his job and coke.

On St. Patrick's Day of 2005, Luke got an unexpected phone call. The message chilled him to his core. "Tomorrow you will come to the alley—"

Luke slammed the phone down.

Jesus. With the whirlwind craziness, he'd completely forgotten the spooky old bitch. He was due back in the Tenderloin the next night, back at that scary dark alley with its magical blank box and...what? He didn't know. It didn't matter because he wasn't going. No way. He ignored the phone's ring several times throughout the night.

The next morning, Luke called in to his assistant at Double B & A, planning to take off sick, stay at home all day and night, out of harm's way.

"Glad you called, Luke," Jamie said. "Got this nutty phone call early this morning on your unlisted private line. Sounded like an old lady, someone with a husky voice, anyhow. Left a cryptic message."

"What'd she say?" he whispered hoarsely.

"Well, it doesn't make any sense to me," Jamie replied. "But she said that either you write in the box or she'd be erasing words. Weird, huh?"

He didn't say anything for a few moments, just stood there with the phone to his ear. His hand wouldn't stop trembling.

"You still there, Luke?"

He cleared his throat. "Yeah, Jamie. Thanks. Don't worry about the call. Probably just some kook, you know?"

"Right."

No matter what, the old lady's deal had really worked for him. The words had indeed been magical. He didn't want her, whoever she was, doing anything that would upset the momentum. No, he'd be there at 11:35 like he'd agreed, write whatever she wanted him to in that fucking box.

The fog was exceptionally thick, making the denizens of the Tenderloin appear out of the mist on O'Farrell like apparitions. Even with the collar of his blue herringbone sport coat pulled up against the cold, Luke shivered as he quickly bypassed the ghostly figures and approached the fuzzy yellow light of the Corner Mart. There, waiting in the fog, stood the bag lady, peering at him with her strange eyes. He had hoped that somehow she wouldn't show.

"Are you ready to write for me, Lucas Somerville?" she asked, moving closer.

He nodded.

"Come, then."

Luke followed her into the alley, chilled to the bone in the foggy darkness, his heart thumping and his blood racing.

At the end of the alley, the old woman stopped and produced a felt-tipped pen and a very thin black book from somewhere in her layers of garments. She handed the pen to Luke.

"Now, you copy the old words from the book."

She had opened the tattered book to a page, its border decorated with symbols akin to those around the box on the wall. It contained only one short sentence.

Luke took the pen and squinted in the dim light at the unfamiliar words: *Te adzari mazzeki O.* Then, with cold, stiff fingers, he slowly transferred the expression into the blank rectangle.

The bag lady murmured, "*Akana mukav tut le Devlesa,*" as she backed slowly away. "I now leave you to God," she repeated in English. At that moment the box on the wall seemed to flare up as if on fire. Simultaneously, Luke thought he heard the sound of lightning ripping through dry air behind him.

He pitched forward, his forehead striking the brick wall and his legs sagging as he collapsed into semi-consciousness.

Minutes later, a tall, dark young woman dressed in a stylish blue herringbone jacket paused after emerging onto O'Farrell from the alley. She blinked in the glare of the streetlight and rubbed her unmatched eyes—one blue, the other brown—then glanced around and smiled broadly, feeling very young and alive.

Meanwhile, back at the end of the alley, an old man sat on a piece of cardboard, staring with a stunned expression into a broken mirror he'd dug out of his nearby shopping cart. He rubbed his arthritic fingers above his left eye as if trying to erase the thin silver slash cutting through his dark eyebrow. After a minute or so, the strong reek of stale urine made his nostrils twitch, partially clearing his head. He traced the deeply etched wrinkles in his face, looked down at his scruffy clothes, and finally stared at the liver-spotted back of his gnarly hand as it gradually dawned on him what the bag woman had done with her magic words. Then, feeling a brief surge of hope, the old man murmured, "The book. I must find that black book," as he searched frantically in the surrounding debris.

He never found it.

TOMBSTONES IN HIS EYES

Junkies are hip,
sometimes bold,
often cool,
but never old.
—graffito in the Haight

Richie O'Brien was in a hurry; a *big* hurry.

A summer fog had blown in from San Francisco Bay as evening settled, cooling off the city, but Richie's body was covered with a sweaty film that made his crotch and underarms feel gritty. His stomach was queasy, his bowels loose, and as he hiked up Powell into Chinatown, the muscles in his legs and arms began to ache as if they would cramp any moment.

Hurry, man, hurry, his limbs screamed silently, a mute chorus of pain.

For most of the morning, he had roamed the Haight in vain, surreptitiously checking the insides of cars, looking for something to boost. Finally, about eleven, he spotted a Fujiko camera in the back seat of a white Topaz, the window cracked down nearly an inch. He glanced about to make sure no one was watching, then had the door open in a few seconds with a wire coat hanger. It was closed again even more quickly. Feeling paranoid about the camera under his shirt, he watched a couple cross the street and stroll his way. They passed by and paid him no mind, so Richie joined a group of punk rockers moving the opposite direction, only partially restraining a giggle of triumph.

When at last he reached the A-1 Pawnshop on Mission Street, it was almost noon, and the Russian had a long line of people waiting to see him. Richie joined the end of the line, and soon, like most of the others ahead of him, he began to squirm, feeling uncomfortable, his crotch itching as if he'd picked up a case of crabs along with the camera. Ahead in line, a few others were even further gone than Richie, hopping back and forth on their feet, smoking one cigarette after another; some were even popping pills and swallowing them dryly. Richie wished he had some codeine or Valium to keep his jones at bay. Like some of the others in line, he hadn't fixed since the night before.

After forty-five minutes or so, it was finally his turn.

"Fif-teen dol-lars," announced the heavyset Russian in the wire cage after examining the Fujiko and looking up with his steely grey eyes.

"Ah, man," Richie complained, his heart sinking, but he knew it was no use arguing. The Russian *never* negotiated with his early customers. He'd just shrug when one indignantly demanded more money, push the item back, and gesture for the next one in line to bypass the disgruntled customer. Richie snatched up the receipt and money, hustling out of the pawnshop past half a dozen people still in line. Some of them looked pretty strung out.

On the sidewalk, Richie bit the knuckle of his right forefinger, thinking hard. He still needed ten bucks to score a quarter gram of Mexican Tar.

"Yeah!" he shouted to himself, remembering the fake Muni fast passes Rudy Sanchez had given him the previous weekend. Rudy, Richie's boyhood friend who worked in a print shop on Castro, always had some scheme for turning a quick buck and usually included Richie in his plots. Right after high school, Richie had taken a fall when a Sanchez scheme turned sour, getting himself ninety days but not ratting out on his friend. During the ten years since, Rudy had often demonstrated his gratitude.

Richie dug out his wallet, unwrapping the cellophane from the ten fast passes. He'd sell two, and he'd be in business. Grinning, he took off for Market Street, deciding on the stop at Tenth.

On the Muni Island, he looked over the four people standing on the median, waiting for a bus. Richie decided to hit up the guy in the plaid sport jacket reading the green section of the Chronicle. Just before he flashed the phony pass, Richie saw a cop waiting to cross Market, looking in their direction. He decided to move back a stop uptown before trying to make a sale.

Richie hit up a dozen or so people before he finally sold two passes. *Guess I gotta work on my sales technique,* he told himself, shrugging off the lack of immediate success as he headed north.

By the time he reached the Cajun's flat off Eddy and Jones in the Tenderloin, Richie was still in pretty good shape. His nose was running a little and he felt the hint of a cramp in the pit of his stomach, but he would be okay after he did some business with his connection.

No one answered the knock at the second floor door. Strange. The Cajun was always home, or his lady, Sweet Jane, was—even holidays. They were both carrying major joneses and needed to take regular care of a large number of customers daily to feed their own habits. But even though he was a heavy user, the Cajun was a good connection; he always gave fair weight, and he and Sweet Jane never cut the tar. Not like those dope fiend assholes over on Sixteenth who worked the street, selling four balloons for one free one from their connections. Those balloons *never* weighed out to a quarter gram, and were sometimes cut with who knew what. You always had to be alert that you were actually getting good shit and not being ripped off. Besides the hassle, it was really easy to get busted doing business out on the street.

No, Richie knew he was lucky to have the Cajun for a safe connection.

He waited, sitting on the top step of the landing, noticing the faint but unmistakable odor of urine in the hallway, and getting edgier and edgier as the afternoon waned. Funny no one else had shown up to score their evening fix. Richie stood and stretched out his legs, which were beginning to get more than just a little stiff. Finally, he sucked in a deep breath, almost gagging on the nearly forgotten smell, and went back to the door to knock again. *Maybe they were asleep the first time,* he told himself, grasping at an explanation. *Bang, bang, bang.*

But no one answered the door this time, either.

He knew he had to do something soon. Even if it meant taking his chances over on Mission and Sixteenth.

"Yo, Richie," said a voice at the bottom of the staircase. "'Sup, man."

It was Short Stuff, a legless black dude who made his way around the Tenderloin on a scooterboard. Short Stuff always knew what was happening.

"Say, Double S," Richie replied, walking down a couple of steps, "you seen the Cajun or his squeeze, man?" He could feel the sweat beginning to trickle down both sides of his ribcage from under his arms.

"Nobody be seeing them two for a while, man," Short Stuff answered. "They busted."

"What do you mean?" Richie said. "The narcs got 'em?" He hoped he was wrong.

"Tha's right," the legless man said, a sympathetic expression on his round black face.

"Oh, man," Richie said, unable to restrain the despair in his voice.

"Say, Richie, why don't ya try the dealer they calls Doom?" Short Stuff suggested.

Richie moved down the remaining steps. "I don't know him."

"Chinatown dude," Short Stuff explained, exchanging a hand-shake as Richie reached ground level and bent over. "He supposed to be doin' that good white shit, man. 'Bout same price as tar."

"Where's he set up?" Richie asked. An edge crept into his tone as his spirits lifted.

"Chinatown...one of 'em tourist minivans, parked upper Powell someplace, just 'fore the cable car turn." He jerked on Richie's pant leg. "But they say you don't wanna fuck with the man call Doom, ya unnerstan'?"

Richie nodded. "I got you, Double S." He slapped the man's raised hand. "I'm light now, my man, but I owe you a shooter of Jack Daniels."

"All right!"

Richie hurried up Powell, the T-shirt under his ragged Giants windbreaker completely soaked and sticking to his back as darkness settled over the city, the unusually thick fog shrouding even the street lights. The tourists had thinned out by this time; only a pair of couples waited for the cable car at the corner to take them back down to Fisherman's Wharf.

He slowed his pace after reaching Washington, where he spotted a black Chrysler minivan with all its side windows shaded. *That's it, man*, he thought.

"Say, homes, 'sup?" a huge black man asked.

He scared the shit out of Richie, appearing from the dark alley like that. Richie had known there would be lookouts, maybe even bodyguards, but he'd expected them to be Asian gang members. The black giant was out of context. In his frantic state of mind, Richie didn't dwell on it. He'd have dealt with Frankenstein's monster to get to his connection.

"Come to see the man," Richie replied after regaining his composure. He nodded at the minivan but didn't take his eyes off the guard, who was picking his teeth with the point of a pocket knife. His face bore the marks of a prize fighter—a flattened nose and scar tissue around both eyebrows.

"That right? Hmmmm…whatcha wanna see him for?" His voice was soft, the words slurred and almost soothing, at odds with his intimidating size and features.

"Business," Richie snapped, growing even more edgy, shifting his weight from one leg to the other and trying to kick out the aching kinks.

"I see."

The big man folded the thin blade and put it away, flashing the butt of an automatic in his belt. "Y'all sweatin', homes. How come? It ain't hot."

"Not feeling too good, man, you know what I mean?" Richie said, wiping his nose and sniffing.

The guy finally nodded, then moved backward into the darkness of the alley, gesturing for Richie to follow. "How much bidness y'all got planned?"

Richie followed a step or two, keeping a little space between them. "A quarter," he replied, holding up one finger.

"Lemme see the bread."

Richie dug out the ten and three fives, holding them out front where the man could see.

"'Kay. Open your coat and 'sume the position, there." He pointed to the dirty brick wall.

Richie did as told, unbuttoning his windbreaker, spreading his feet, and leaning up against the wall.

The man frisked him quickly and thoroughly, even brushing his groin.

"Turn 'round."

Richie turned about, noticing a flashlight in the black man's hand.

"'Kay, push up both sleeves, homes…wanna see some history."

Richie pushed up the sleeves of his windbreaker, exposing his bare arms to the strong flashlight beam.

The man reached out and roughly fingered Richie's track marks, halting at the fresh bruise on his right inner elbow. "Alright, this way." He gestured with the flashlight for Richie to follow him to the minivan. He unlocked the side door but warned, "Be cool, y'all hear?" before he opened the door.

"Thank you, Sandman," a dry voice whispered from inside the vehicle.

Something about the sound made the short hairs prickle on Richie's neck as he slipped through the door to find the middle seats removed. He squatted on the floor as the door slid shut, immediately clasping his arms around himself. The temperature in the back of the minivan had to be thirty or forty degrees lower than outside. *No air conditioning is this good,* Richie thought, shivering.

In the dim light from one overhead bulb, Richie stared at a tiny man seated across from him on the rear seat, his face partially shadowed. He could see that the man wore a wispy Fu Manchu mustache, but face didn't really appear young or old—just Asian. The little man was dressed in black: a square satin-lined hat and matching high-necked robe. His hands were crossed in front of him, disappearing into the long, wide sleeves of the gown. On the left breast of the robe was embroidered a white snow dragon, its wings folded but talons extended, its fanged mouth open and its gaze fierce—a striking adornment against the all-black background.

"You name?" the man asked. The whispery, abbreviated English had a quality of implied threat, reminding Richie of the burring of a rattlesnake. He shivered again, trying to rub some warmth into his arms.

"Richie O'Brien," he whispered back, thinking, *Jesus, man, turn up the heat.*

The man in black nodded. "You call me Mis-ter Doom."

Richie wondered if the name was Chinese or English.

The interrogation continued. "You customer of...?"

"The Cajun in the Tenderloin."

Still no expression on his face, the little man nodded.

"You do business now with me." It was more of a statement than a question.

Richie nodded.

"You habit...how much a day?"

"Quarter wakeup, quarter nighttime," Richie answered, wiping his nose.

"Money?"

Richie dug out his twenty-five dollars.

The man nodded, withdrew his hands from the sleeves of his black robe, and reached for the bills. He took the money in his right hand, twisted, and slipped it into a concealed cubbyhole in the minivan's upholstery. In his other hand, he held two little cellophane bags containing small amounts of white powder. "This best grade China White, thirty dollar quarter gram. But, new customer special. Two quarter gram for you, Mis-ter ah-Brien, twenty-five dollar." He ran both title and name together, inflecting the last syllable.

Richie reached for the baggies.

Mr. Doom snatched both away.

"So sorry, just *one* for now," he said, leaning forward and handing Richie one baggie. "I know what happen if you take both. All gone tonight. Come back here tomorrow morning. I not here, but Sandman, he give you other one." The second baggie was no longer in his hand, and Richie would have sworn it had just disappeared into the frigid air. The man leaned forward, extending his empty, long-fingered, delicate hand for a formal shake.

Richie leaned forward, too, taking the man's hand in his, unable to restrain another shiver. Mr. Doom's hand was colder than if it had been sculpted from a cake of ice.

But it was the little man's eyes that Richie found truly disturbing: no iris, almost all pupil. And they weren't round. No, they appeared to be arched and squared off at the bottom, a shape vaguely familiar. As the little man sat back, his face again in shadow, Richie shrugged off the unnerving feeling, telling himself the weird eye shape was only a trick of the dim light.

"Goodbye, Mis-ter ah-Brien. *I* see you tomorrow night."

He was back on the street, standing by the ex-fighter, Sandman.

"See you, tomorrow morning," Richie said, hurrying away down Powell.

"'Kay, homes," Sandman replied in his soft voice.

At the almost-empty flat he shared with Lisha in the Haight, Richie dug out his rig from under the mattress on the floor and cooked up the China White with trembling fingers. He didn't even turn on a lamp, instead working by the light glaring through the bedroom window from a streetlight on Broderick. He almost forgot about the recent nightmares he'd had while nodding—

"Whoa," he said to himself, remembering at the last moment. The bad dreams had seemed more like…an alternate reality. It was getting harder to wake up, to come back out of them. Before fixing, he got Lisha's cooking timer and set it for fifteen minutes. He hoped it would help bring him off the dope nod, draw him back to the bedroom from…wherever.

Oh, yeah!

Mr. Doom's shit was righteous, grabbing his stomach quickly but gently then sending wave after wave of stone-ass calm tingling through his body and finally smoothing out the kinks in his arms and legs. His eyelids grew heavy and sagged. He was drifting away to a rhythmic beat.

Tick, tick, tick.

It is night. Clouds blot out the moon and stars. But more than just dark, the city colors have disappeared, replaced by charcoals, indigos, and blacks—lots of blacks. There is a peculiar lack of night sound; no sirens, no cars, no shouting, no laughing. Nothing. Completely still. It is more than the sense of experiencing a quiet, dark night; the complete black silence is unsettling. You find yourself standing, squinting, and peering down the mouth of an alley, the nearby streetlight out. It is like staring into the abyss. You shiver, even though it isn't an especially cold night. No, but you have a compelling need to search this alley, this black, forbidding spot; it is this compulsion to step into the unknown that makes you shiver.

Why?

You don't remember. You have no explanation for this need, no clue of what may lie ahead.

You take several tentative steps into the blackness, your right hand lightly touching the brick wall on the right side as a guide. You stop, sucking in several deep breaths, trying to calm your racing pulse. After a moment or two, your eyes adjust to the blackness, and you are able to make out things on your side of the alley for a few feet ahead. You move forward cautiously, keeping your hand in contact with the wall, which feels grimy, filthy. After a few more steps you come to the first of the garbage cans lining this side of the alley. Careful not to touch or rattle the cans, you slip around the obstacles. A few more steps and you become acutely aware of a smell, a clinging, sweet smell of decay—the familiar smell of something dead. It hangs in the air, growing stronger as you move deeper into the darkness. By now, you can just see across the alley to the other brick wall. Along that side there are a few cans, but mostly stacks of cardboard boxes.

In the dark ahead, just out of sight, you hear something move.

Not a footstep, nothing human like that. No, it's more like something brushing lightly against a cardboard box, a furtive sound, animal-like. You pause, cock your head, and listen carefully, straining to hear the sound again, searching for another movement from whatever lurks ahead.

Nothing.

Except for the cloying odor of death.

You shiver again but plod ahead, forcing yourself to take each careful step, compelled by some deep inner need. You move out away from the right wall, cautiously treading the center of the narrow alley.

The sound comes again, and it raises the short hairs on your neck.

You have no idea what type of creature would make such a sound, but you have the sense it is something very dangerous. Overwhelming panic saps the strength from your legs and loosens your bowels.

You are terrified.

Straining, you try to penetrate the darkness ahead, to locate the source. It is too dark.

Then, as if in response to your need, the clouds part slightly and the moon illuminates the remaining length of alley, its angle shadowing only the last three feet or so.

It is a dead end, and you strain to penetrate the darkness at the very back.

Nothing. There is nothing there.

The alley is empty.

A paper bag, pushed free by a sporadic breeze, separates from a pile of cardboard in the shadows and tumbles along past you, making the strange sound. You breathe a sigh of relief.

But then you realize that you are alone at the dead end…trapped if something enters the alley now.

The gap in the clouds closes, shrouding the moon. A wave of panic overwhelms you in the sudden darkness.

Gasping for breath, you struggle to regain control of your senses, calm your thumping heart. Your pulse rate slowly drops down. Then, at the moment you seem back in control of yourself, you feel that creepy intuitive sense of being spied upon.

Someone is watching you.

You must get out. You turn and stumble back toward the dim light at the mouth of the alley, looking about frantically for a window, a doorway, trying to locate the person watching. There is nothing. The mouth of the alley seems so far away, so far. You try to run; your legs are still rubbery but finally respond to your will. In the back of your mind you are pleading silently: where is it, that sound that will draw me back?

Run, run, run, faster.

You stop, spotting the silhouette in the mouth of the alley. A man, a huge man, just standing and watching.

Then: running! The faint sound punches through the darkness.

And you are being pulled back, back, back.

Rinnnng!

Lisha's timer was ringing, a jarring, grating sound, but so welcome and wonderful.

Richie sat up as the ringing ceased, the sheet over him soaked with sweat. *Jesus, that was so real,* he thought. Where was that place—a place where the blackness of night settled and smothered all sound?

* * *

The next morning, Richie returned from Chinatown early and
fixed again.

The nightmare in the alley recurred, but this time the feeling
of being watched was so strong that almost from the moment he
entered the alley, he felt like someone was stalking him.

Who? And why? He didn't know for sure, but he continually
glanced back at the mouth of the alley, expecting to see the giant
silhouette again. No one was ever there.

Finally, the timer pulled him back to safety.

Later, Richie rinsed away the dried sweat of fear. He stepped
out of the shower physically clean, but his mind remained unsettled by the nightmare.

Wrapped in a towel, he made his way into the kitchen and
stopped at the table. There were two chocolate doughnuts sitting
on a folded piece of paper. He took a bite of one of the doughnuts and opened the note:

Richie,

    Ice cream in the freezer.

    Miss you, but you got to get clean. I talked to your
mom and told her about the farm. She'll get most of the
money. Aunt Elva will help with the rest. You can do it,
like me. It's going good, a day at a time.

Love you.

Lisha

A month or so ago before he'd hocked most of their furniture, Lisha had bailed out on him, going to her Aunt El in the
Sunset. With the old lady's financial help, she had entered a treatment program up in Glen Ellen at Truman's Mountain Vista
Farm, where she'd apparently gotten her mind right. She had been
back from the farm at Aunt El's for about five days, but had
called him only once. She had told him she had a sponsor now

and was working a twelve-step program. She said she couldn't see him until he was clean. A few days ago she'd left a receipt for the paid rent.

Richie made himself a milkshake with the ice cream Lisha had left. He washed down the other chocolate doughnut with the thick drink. *Holy crap*, he thought, *she's blown the whistle to my mom.* His mother had thought everything was cool since Lisha and he had gone through the methadone detox program back in December. What a joke. Each day they'd cut back the dosage at the clinic. As they had gotten down to where they could feel the new jones kicking in—about day twenty-six—they'd both started using shit again. And kept using steady for the next six months, until the day that had shaken Lisha so badly she had taken the action to get herself straight.

He was strung out that day, pretty bad, missing a fix the night before and not scoring that morning, but keeping his jones at bay with codeine and Valium. Finally, he sold a pair of boosted car stereos to a fence he knew for twenty dollars and got enough tar for a short fix for both him and Lisha. With all the codeine and Valium in his system, he quit breathing right after shooting up. Lisha, scared shitless and shaky herself, dumped him in front of emergency at San Francisco General and sped off in her beat-up VW bug.

The next thing Richie knew, he was staring up into a nurse's face.

"That's right," she said, a mixed expression on her face—half relief, half disgust, "you overdosed on heroin. We gave you a shot of Narcon, an opiate blocker. You're going to be okay, this time."

"Water?" he asked hoarsely, realizing he was on a gurney in the hallway just outside the emergency room.

Nearby, another guy was stretched out, a hand on his bandaged head, moaning, "The muthahfuckah kicked me."

The nurse nodded and said, "You stay put, I'll be back in a second."

As soon as she disappeared through a nearby door, he got up and took off, hustling quickly out of the hospital even though his legs were rubbery and he still felt badly shaken.

* * *

Richie finished the milkshake, mulling it all over in his head, trying to think clearly. It was hard.

He knew he should quit, but at the farm? Man, that'd be almost like going to the slam. And all that higher power jazz in the steps that Lisha was so stoked on. Giving yourself up to God?

No way, man.

He could do it himself, real soon. Maybe even tomorrow. Yeah, why not? Tomorrow, he'd kick.

Absently, Richie flipped on Lisha's answering machine. He'd tried to hock it the week before, but it was so old the Russian wouldn't give him anything for it, not even a five spot. But it still worked well enough for him to hear the excitement in Rudy Sanchez's voice:

"Yo, Richie. Got to see you, man—" There was a pause and Richie thought his friend was restraining a giggle. "Got a deal, a big one this time. Call me at the print shop or come by at four, when I get off. Do it, man, our ship has finally come in. This is the big one!"

Richie grinned to himself. Another scheme. He wondered what this one would be. He had no idea, but he would be over at the print shop on Castro to cash in when Sanchez got off.

There was another message on the machine.

"Richie, this is your mother. Oh, Richie how could you do it again? You said the methadone program was ninety percent successful. But Lisha has told me the whole story…" She paused long enough that Richie was about to turn the machine off, then he heard, "Son, this thing Lisha has gone through can work. That farm's a good place. She's sure. I'm sure. And I can get most of the money right now. Lisha says her aunt will loan us the rest, until I can refinance the house. You've got to go up there to that program. Please say yes, Richie. Call me today. I love you, son."

For a moment, Richie had a twinge of shame.

He'd conned his mother out of hundreds, maybe thousands, of dollars—*Just this month, Ma, to help with the rent*—until she'd found out what he and Lisha had really been doing with the money. Even then she had paid for the methadone treatment. But she'd gotten smart, making out the check for three hundred and eighty to the clinic and giving it to them directly.

Okay, Mom, he pledged silently, *tonight will be it.* He raised his hand in a kind of sworn pledge gesture.

I'm going to kick. Tomorrow.

That was it. Official.

He sighed, checking the clock: 2:50.

Better get it together and hustle over to Sanchez's. He needed some bread before he could see Mr. Doom for the last time.

"Come in here a minute, Richie," Rudy said, gesturing to the bathroom at the back of the print shop, his dark eyes shiny with excitement. "You ain't going to believe this, man."

Richie wiped his nose, glanced back at the two employees and the waiting customers, then followed his friend into the little restroom.

Rudy locked the door, reached into his shirt, and brought out a brown paper bag. He slipped his hand in and withdrew two bundles of money, each held tightly with a thick rubber band. He thumbed through one roll of bills. They were all twenties. "Take it, man, that one is yours."

Dumbfounded, Richie took it, thumbing the bills himself.

"Twenty-five in each bundle," Rudy announced. "Five hundred bucks, man. Go on, count yours."

Richie fingered the bundle, counting the twenties. He glanced up at his friend. "There's twenty-five all right."

"And...?"

Richie shrugged. "And what? There are twenty-five twenties here...five hundred dollars, right?"

Rudy giggled. "It's funny money, man."

"Counterfeit?" Richie said, taking a closer look at the top bill. He rubbed it between his fingers. It looked okay, but maybe the green color was off slightly, too dark, and the paper did feel funny, a little slicker than a regular bill.

"Yeah, pretty good, huh?" Rudy said. His face lit up with a big smile. "I only paid fifty bucks for each bundle."

"From who, man?"

Rudy's expression sobered. "You don't need to know that, Richie. If you and I can move this thousand, I can buy a *real* bundle. Ten grand!"

Richie looked down at the bundle of twenties again. "Man, our ship did finally come in."

"Yeah, but you got to hustle, man," Rudy said, stuffing his bundle into his pocket. "We got to push each roll by eleven tomorrow morning. Here's the way I see it: we make small purchases, like a pack of cigarettes at a liquor store, a sandwich at a 7-Eleven, you understand. Get as much change as possible, maybe four hundred fifty or sixty for each roll. Then I can buy the ten grand from my source at noon. You in, man?"

"Hey, I'm in!"

Richie stuffed the wad of twenties into his pants pocket. The memory of the note from Lisha, the phone call from his Mom, and his pledge were already forgotten. This was going to work. No more getting sick, sweating his next fix.

"Okay, let's get busy," Rudy said, unlocking the restroom door. "Meet you at your place tomorrow morning at ten."

Richie nodded and started out the door.

Rudy grabbed his arm, his face uncharacteristically screwed up with concern. "Don't fuck me up on this one, pal. Be at your place at eleven with the good bills."

"Hey, man, I'll be there."

After buying packs of cigarettes at two different convenience stores four blocks apart, Richie realized that it would take some time and hustling to get rid of all twenty-five bills this way. He'd have to cover the whole frigging town. Standing in front of the 7-Eleven, he lit a Winston and inhaled.

Nah, there was a better way, faster. He could turn the remaining bogus four-sixty into even more, make a little profit before seeing Rudy and giving him his four-fifty. Richie grinned to himself.

Yeah!

The black minivan was parked almost in the same spot on

Powell, but there was a lot of foot traffic in Chinatown this early in the evening. Richie waited nervously a block away, smoking and watching, until the foot traffic finally thinned out.

He moved closer.

"Say, homes, 'sup?" said Sandman, stepping out from the nearby alley just like the previous night. He gestured for Richie to follow him back into the darkness.

Richie followed, assuming the position to be frisked. Sandman's hand paused at Richie's front pants pocket and tapped the bundle of phony money.

"Bread?"

Richie nodded, feeling a little rush of adrenaline.

"How much bidness y'all wanna do, homes?"

"Want to buy some wholesale, be the bagman myself," Richie answered, turning around and pulling out the bundle of twenties.

"That right?" Sandman said. Even in the dim light, Richie could read the doubt on his face, but the ex-fighter recovered quickly. "Ya'll score a bank?"

Richie shook his head.

"How much ya holding?"

"Four hundred sixty."

"'Kay. Let me check the man," Sandman said. "Y'all stay put." The big man went over to the minivan and unlocked the side door. He disappeared inside while Richie smoked in the alley. After a minute or so, Sandman emerged from the vehicle and nodded at Richie.

"Y'all in luck, homes," he said, beckoning with one hand. "Mr. Doom says send ya in." He slid the door open. "Be cool."

Now that he was close to making a big deal, Richie's chest tightened and his mouth went dry.

Again, the inside of the van felt like an ice cavern, and Mr. Doom was dressed the same as the night before, all in black. He nodded as Richie sat down on the floor of the vehicle. "Mis-ter ah-Brien. Sandman, he say you want to do real business?"

"Yeah, I want to buy some wholesale."

For the first time since they'd met, Mr. Doom smiled slightly. "Mis-ter ah-Brien, then you be competitor?"

"Not with you, Mr. Doom," Richie said a little too loudly. He was beginning to sweat. "I'll probably work down on Sixteenth, you know, competing with the guys on the street."

"That very dangerous."

Richie forced a smile. "I know, but nothing ventured, nothing gained."

The lack of expression returned to Mr. Doom's face. "How much you expect to buy?" he asked, nodding at Richie's bundle.

"Ten grams?" Richie answered hoarsely, his tongue almost sticking to the roof of his mouth.

Mr. Doom shook his head sadly. "Maybe seven better."

"Okay," Richie agreed, handing over the roll of bogus twenties, the sweat beginning to roll down his sides under his shirt and windbreaker. He knew this was the moment. If Mr. Doom even suspected the money was fake, he'd call Sandman, who would probably haul him into the alley and waste him right there.

To his surprise, Mr. Doom didn't even count the money. He just stuffed it, still banded, into the cache in the upholstered wall of the van. In his hand, he held a large clear bag full of smaller cellophane baggies. "Seven gram," he declared, handing Richie the heroin.

Richie reached out, his hand trembling slightly.

But Mr. Doom didn't let go of the dope. "Partnership built on trust. I trust you?" he asked, the ice in his voice matching the chilling temperature inside the minivan.

Richie nodded vigorously.

The little man released the bag and leaned forward, extending his right hand. "Mis-ter ah-Brien, we partners."

Richie accepted the cold shake, staring into the strange eyes and finally recognizing the shape of the pupils.

Jesus, they were *tombstones*. And it wasn't the light. He swallowed hard, then struggled up into a stooped posture, ready to go.

Mr. Doom grabbed the sleeve of Richie's windbreaker and held him in place with a surprising amount of strength from a person so small. Richie turned back to face him. "Partner cheat, partner gone," Mr. Doom whispered in his creepy burr, the message very clear.

* * *

The night is the same, with all the dark tones, but something about the alley is different. You pause at the mouth, your senses hyper-alert.

It is the smell, of course.

The cloying sweet smell of death hangs heavy in the darkness, almost a tangible thing; you have the feeling that you can almost reach out and touch it, this smell. Still, you force yourself to move forward, one step after another, compelled by some inner need...or something in the alley drawing you to it, like the magnetism between the flute and the cobra. The smell filling your nostrils is so strong that you stop and almost retch.

At that moment you hear something deep in the blackness of the alley, a sound so short in duration you are unable to describe or recall it. It frightens you, nevertheless. Your chest is tight, your limbs stiff. It is only with maximum effort that you are able to force your legs to move. But you do move forward, cautiously, down the middle of the alley, peering into the darkness, the odor forgotten. Again you sense the presence of someone watching you, the feeling making your skin prickle. You turn, half expecting to see the giant at the mouth of the alley. No, nothing. Someone is waiting ahead. Someone who makes the strange, frightening noise.

Carefully, you move deeper and deeper into the quiet, still darkness.

The sound again disturbs the stillness: a short grunt mixed with a throaty cough. Yes, that's it.

An unnatural sound.

You stop as the clouds draw apart, and even the end of the alley is flooded with moonlight. You peer at the dead end, expecting to see the ex-fighter, expecting to peer into the barrel of his gun. You squint, and even in the dim light you realize the bodyguard is not there. No, but there is a shadow, stretching out toward you. As the shadow touches your feet, you feel the temperature instantly plunge and you shiver. Strange...

Another cough-grunt and your gaze is drawn up to the roof of the end wall. You gasp loudly at the source of the shadow and the weird sound.

The dragon!

The snow dragon, clinging to the roof edge like some hideous gargoyle, breathing plumes of steam into the icy atmosphere.

The white monster peers down on you like a hawk staring down at a mouse. In the moonlight, it is terrifying but magnificent, its body shining like the finest alabaster, its penetrating gaze black as ebony. It is the gaze that holds you locked in place as the great creature unfurls its wings. The huge span casts a shadow over most of the alley.

Spellbound, you watch as the creature prepares to leap into the air, its long talons curling and gripping the roof's edge, the tremendous wingspan beating a downblast of icy air that crashes into your face like the wind of an arctic storm.

Rinnng! The sound is faint and distant. Too distant.

The great snow dragon is airborne, circling overhead, gaining momentum. Finally, it is swooping down at you, its fanged mouth open, breathing a fiery ball of tumbling blue.

You are engulfed in the ball of blue flame; an invisible, icy hand crushes the life from your body. But in that last nanosecond of life you smile, recognizing the irony: the dragon has freed you.

Rudy Sanchez broke in and found Richie stretched out on his mattress the next morning, eyes staring into eternity, a surprising smile on his face. Beside Richie on the floor, Rudy found a candle, two empty baggies, a burnt spoon with a cotton ball, a foot of rubber surgical cord, and a hypodermic.

Rudy shook his head, knowing that Richie had finally screwed up once too often. He stared down at his friend, wondering what had caused that smile.

In addition to Richie's smile, there was something else that struck Rudy as odd.

Richie's pupils weren't pinned, the normal condition for a user of opiates. Just the opposite: they were dilated, arched at the top, squared off at the bottom.

"Strange," Rudy whispered aloud.

For Gavin, who has battled the dragon

BUSHIDO

"They are all perfect!"
Katsumoto's final words, *The Last Samurai*

The Ugly Man paused at the mouth of his alley and pulled up the hood of his black sweatshirt. Gathering in the darkness around himself, he stepped out into the foggy night. He shuffled down O'Farrell Street like a wounded panther, limping along under the shadowed overhangs, staying close to the barred and chained storefronts. As usual, none of the denizens of San Francisco's Tenderloin even glanced in his direction. He'd once read, or probably heard, someplace in the distant past that disfigured or ugly—*really* ugly—people, instead of drawing attention, were actually almost invisible. Normal adults looked away, quickly wiping out what they'd glimpsed and passing by as if the ugly person didn't even exist—a subconscious wish fulfillment reaction, perhaps. That had indeed been the Ugly Man's experience in the 'loin. When he managed to avoid making any but cursory eye contact, he moved about in the nighttime shadows with complete anonymity, unacknowledged, unseen, feeling almost like an imaginary creature with no name.

It was long after midnight—the time of heavy buying and selling in the 'loin. Music and laughter blared from seedy bars. The street was littered with empty bottles, plastic wrappers, and discarded food scraps. Those law-abiding residents with an indoor address in the 'loin had long ago disappeared from the streets for the safety behind closed and double-locked doors, leaving a handful of cops and the unsavory crowd of night people. A level of nervous tension hung in the misty air over the mob of shifty-eyed dealers, dead-eyed junkies, heavily mascara-eyed hookers, steely-eyed pimps, and the vacant-eyed homeless, all scurrying about with an agenda like a scattered pack of abandoned dogs scavenging for scraps. The Ugly Man slipped along, bypassing a rheumy wino who argued loudly with an imaginary friend in a littered doorway. He made absolutely no lingering eye contact, avoiding any communication, a disabled phantom of the street.

Usually he avoided the late night crowd in the Tenderloin altogether, but it was the final day of the month, and he had used up the last of his SSI money two days prior. He harbored only a wrinkled dollar bill and a pocketful of change, most of which he'd acquired selling aluminum cans earlier in the evening over in the Mission. His dire financial circumstances had forced him to skip his early morning trip down to Wild Bill's Liquor Store on Leavenworth. He'd delayed his evening trip too long. His hands were shaking badly, his mouth dry and metallic, his body covered with clammy sweat under his clothes despite the penetrating chill that hung in the air. As he dragged his aching right leg along, he felt a growing nausea. Still, he carefully kept to the shadows, shuffling along until the green neon of Wild Bill's glowed fuzzily ahead in the fog. Sighing with relief, the Ugly Man pulled his threadbare black hood down, completely exposing his horribly disfigured features.

At the doorway he paused and glanced down, waiting for a pair of customers to leave the liquor store. Then he limped directly to the counter. The Indian clerk recognized the Ugly Man immediately and announced with a slightly British accent, "Ham and cheese sandwich and pint of Wild Irish Rose, right?"

He shook his head. "No sandwich," he answered in a husky, under-used voice, placing the dollar and a portion of the change on the counter with a noticeably shaking hand. "Only a half pint," he added, swallowing dryly.

The clerk took a step toward the back display, found the correct half pint, and placed it on the counter. Then he scooped up the money, carefully counting the coins before ringing up the sale.

The Ugly Man cleared his throat and asked, "A favor?"

The clerk frowned slightly. "What kind of favor?"

"Use one of those," the Ugly Man said, then added a barely audible, "please." He pointed at a triangle of dusty souvenir shot glasses stacked on the counter, but mostly hidden behind the plastic cigarette lighter display.

The clerk just stared at him with a kind of puzzled expression after glancing at the stack. He tentatively picked up the shot glass from atop the pyramid.

"Now fill it, please," the Ugly Man said, nodding toward his half pint of whisky. "I can't."

Understanding finally flooded into the clerk's face and dark eyes after glancing at the shot glass and then down at the Ugly Man's badly trembling hand. He shook his head and explained in a bureaucratic monotone, "I am sorry, but we are not allowed to uncap any bottle, open any can, or dispense alcoholic drinks of any kind on the premises, because we would jeopardize our off sale liquor license."

"It'll only take a moment, then I'll disappear," the Ugly Man pleaded in a pitiful whisper.

The clerk, looking uncomfortably torn, glanced out the doorway and then back at the Ugly Man. Despite his obvious misgivings, he uncapped the bottle of whisky and poured out a generous portion, filling the shot glass right to the top. He pushed it across the counter and whispered, "Quickly," glancing nervously again at the empty doorway. "*You* poured it, if anyone comes in," he warned. He left the counter and stepped back into the rear of the store, near the cold cases, wiping his hands as if disowning any part of the illegal transaction.

The Ugly Man breathed in and out deeply, gathered himself, then reached down and encircled the glass ever so carefully, keeping his shaking hands firmly grounded against the counter as if he were attempting to gently restrain a baby bird from flying off. During the process, his coat pulled up, exposing the lower several inches of his tattooed sleeves, the mosaic badly disfigured by thickly layered burn scars. Sucking in another breath to further steady himself, he leaned over and slurped from the glass, which still rested firmly on the counter between his grounded hands. He closed his eyes, swallowed the raw whisky, and held his breath as the fiery liquid made its way down to his stomach. After a moment, he blinked, shuddered, and carefully lifted the shot glass with his still slightly trembling hands. He only spilled a few drops of the precious liquid before downing the remainder of the poured drink. Licking his dry lips, he nodded toward the clerk as he set the empty glass back down. "Thanks, man," he said. He picked up and carefully capped the remaining half pint of Wild Irish Rose.

Stepping into the doorway, the Ugly Man looked about

furtively while secreting his purchase in the pocket of his scruffy sweatshirt. He could already feel the "medicine" beginning to take effect, settling his stomach. A warm glow slowly worked its way out to his extremities, even quelled the almost constant ache in his lower right leg.

Feeling better, he made his way back up the street, heading home to his cardboard tent.

As he neared an apartment entryway just before reaching O'Farrell, the Ugly Man heard a loud skin-on-skin *smack*, followed by snuffled crying.

He stopped, tilted his head, and cautiously peeked into the back of the deep, darkened doorway.

There was Mad Marco, the badass bald-headed pimp, dressed in his expensive black leather coat, holding up and waving a pair of wrinkled ten-dollar bills in his left hand. "I warned you earlier, you lazy bitch, didn't I?"

A scantily dressed young woman fingered a bloody nose. She shivered visibly in the cold, nodding contritely.

"Now, you get your raggedy ass out there and hustle up at least another hundred bucks before morning, you understand me?" Mad Marco said, pulling up his leather coat and pointing at a wide metal-studded belt. "If you don't, you know what I'm gonna have to do?"

The bleeding woman nodded, murmuring, "Don't do that, Marco. I'm sorry."

"Sorry?" the scowling pimp repeated angrily. "Sorry don't hack it, girl. You get out there and shake your lazy-ass booty, get them johns' noses opened up, attract some bidness, you hear?" He paused a moment, then ordered, "Here, clean yourself up."

The young woman took a powder blue silk handkerchief from the pimp and wiped at her bloody nose. Stoically, she sucked it up, trying to smile and put on her game face while still shivering. She looked to be sixteen years old at best. Most others like her would be begging for spare change over in the Haight or maybe streetwalking on Capp Street. There were few fresh-faced, bright-eyed hookers in the 'loin. She should be making a ton of money, the Ugly Man thought. Maybe that was what pissed off Mad Marco. The girl might be too timid to really exploit her innocent assets and hustle up customers. Could even be her first night on the street. He didn't recall having ever seeing her before, but he usually paid little attention to the hookers, regardless their ages or innocence.

It was none of his business anyhow. Glancing away, the Ugly Man slipped past the darkened doorway unnoticed.

Maybe sometime in the past he would have intervened, back during the good times when he'd practiced the Seven Virtues and still had some self-respect and his night watchman job over at the warehouses in China Basin. But he'd been fired nine or ten years ago, after the accident, when he'd been discovered asleep and drunk on the job. He smiled wryly to himself as he limped along, shaking his head. Thinking about it, he wasn't sure he'd have said anything, not even back then. Probably just idle fancy.

He glanced absently up the darkened street, reflecting back.

Even as a child in the Napa Valley he'd been reclusive, avoiding most interpersonal conflict. In his heart, he knew it wasn't in his nature to have risked Mad Marcus's wrath any time in the distant past, much less the present. The pimp was scary tough, always carried a straight razor, and was known to use it with the least provocation.

No, the Ugly Man admitted to himself, slinking off into the fog like a cowardly dog with its tail between its hind legs. *Mind your own business, stay invisible, take care of number one, stay out of harm's way.* That was his credo now. He hadn't even thought about the Seven Virtues for years.

After leaving the two in the entryway with only the briefest twinge of guilt, he turned up O'Farrell and spotted Shaky Jake; the old man's Parkinson's disease twitched his hands and head almost out of control.

"Man, I take anything, even a penny," the Vietnam vet said in a slurred voice, trying to panhandle change from a hooded, out-of-service parking meter. He obviously hadn't been over to the VA clinic recently to renew his meds.

Impulsively, the Ugly Man dug out the remaining change

from his pocket—a dime, four nickels, and seven pennies. In an uncharacteristic charitable move, perhaps stimulated by his lingering guilt at not helping the under-age hooker, he slipped the coins into the trembling hand of the hallucinating old man. "There you go, Jake," he said, before limping off up the street.

A few moments later, he became acutely aware of a sharp tingling and itching sensation all over his skin. At the time, he didn't recognize it as anything special. He figured it was just another symptom of alcohol withdrawal, like the shakes, or maybe it had something to do with the drying up of his clammy skin. He told himself that the discomfort would disappear as soon as he had a chance to drink the remainder of the Wild Irish Rose and towel off. He hurried along, ignoring both the funny skin sensation and the nagging ache in his right leg.

Safely back in the cardboard tent at the dead end of an alley just down from Van Ness on O'Farrell, the Ugly Man drained the remainder of the Wild Irish Rose in three long, satisfying pulls. He wiped the tears from his eyes. The effects of the cheap whisky kicked in immediately, warming him to his core and lifting his spirits.

Slowly, he undressed to the waist, exposing the frail, undernourished body of an old man to the night chill. He was only thirty-eight. As he wiped down his naked skin with an old towel, he paid little attention to the tattooed mosaic that decorated his arms and body. It had been badly disfigured by the burn scars, but he was concerned only with the itching along both arms and across his chest and back. It was driving him nuts. He rubbed the towel briskly along his right arm, some of the skin sloughing away onto the towel. The Ugly Man stopped and stared incredulously at his arm. Remarkably, the scars appeared to be fading away, the brilliant colors of the once-blemished tattoos seeming to again take prominence. He checked the other arm: same thing, the scars shrinking away. But that couldn't be. The doctors had said he was permanently scarred. He took out a cracked mirror remnant from his meager pile of belongings and examined his face, where he'd been most badly burned.

Jesus, he swore silently. The heavy scar tissue had indeed diminished noticeably. Impossible.

Maybe he'd finally gone around the corner, after all the years of heavy boozing and not taking care of himself. He peered intently into the mirror again, confirming the startling change and fingering the shrunken disfigurement.

The Ugly Man stood and hastily stripped off his double pairs of pants. The lighter scars overlaying the tattoos on his legs were almost entirely gone. Shivering in the unheated cardboard tent, he hesitated only a moment before pulling his pants back on. He hurriedly slipped on his shirts and sat back down, stunned. Something strange was going on, some kind of transformation; his skin was changing back to like it had been before the fiery attack in the park in the Haight, looking exactly as it had when he'd been elegantly tattooed by his friend Rembrandt. So long ago...

When he finally left the Napa Valley in his mid twenties, he moved to a studio apartment on Stanyon in the Haight, found a night watchman job, and fairly soon thereafter met the famous dwarf tat-master, Rembrandt. They both ate in the late afternoon at the Crescent Cafe on Haight, soon becoming unlikely friends—the backward, shy young man from the country listening, the outgoing, hip dwarf from the city talking. Rembrandt was so artistically talented he'd spent the previous eighteen months in Tokyo doing full-body tattooing at the exclusive Red Crane. In his off hours, he studied Japanese history, focusing on the Samurai period.

In those first few months after becoming tight friends, the tat-master covered his awed friend with traditional Japanese-style mythological tattoos. He used intricate, colorful floral designs interlaced with strange creatures and demons on the young man's arms and legs. A work of art that would have cost tens of thousands of dollars at the Red Crane, the center piece finished last on the young man's back was an iridescent dragon that wove in and out of chrysanthemums and long-nosed, wide-eyed demons, looking back squarely with a fearsome red-eyed frown.

"I've accurately captured the ancient pattern, dude," Rembrandt said reverently, finally setting down the tattooing needles after the last session. "Now you must adhere to *Bushido*." He bowed formally. "Follow the Way of the Warrior, observe the Seven Virtues like I do: Rectitude—right dealing, Courage—respect and caution replace fear, Benevolence—aiding others, Respect—courtesy to all, Honesty—conscience, Loyalty—responsibility to self and others, and Honor—above all. If you can maintain the Way, your life will be transformed."

He bowed again, and as an afterthought, whispered, "Your spirit is eternally protected by a magical web now, the dragon vigilantly guarding your back."

Remarkably, the prophecy started to come true. The young man began to emerge from his shyness, meeting people more easily—even girls—gaining confidence and self-esteem. He even received an outstanding performance report at work.

Then, the terrible accident.

The young man was driving himself and the tat-master home after a wonderful party on the peninsula with a group of Rembrandt's fans. He suddenly lost control on Highway 101 near Candlestick Park. The Volkswagen Bug flipped over and over, shearing off a highway sign, crashing against a power pole, and igniting into flame. Miraculously unhurt, the young man scrambled from the car, leaving his unconscious friend trapped in the burning wreck. Too frightened to risk a rescue, afraid the vehicle was going to explode at any minute, he stood by and did nothing.

Rembrandt never regained consciousness. Six hours later, he died from the injuries at UCSF Hospital.

Even after so many years, the guilt-ridden Ugly Man had a catch in his tightened throat when he thought about his only true friend. He'd squandered so much in his cowardice. He sighed, wishing he had another half pint to help him get through the night, and crawled under his raggedy blankets, trying to relax and fall asleep. But his rest was disturbed by the memory of his own fiery attack in the park.

Soon after his friend had died and he'd lost his job and apartment on Stanyon, the Ugly Man had been forced to move into a pup tent in Buena Vista Park in the lower Haight, living near the other homeless people back in the heavy brush and trees. One night, six months or so after moving there, he had been attacked by a gang of teenage thieves, robbed, beaten with a baseball bat, doused with barbecue fluid, and set afire. His right fibula had been shattered, his face and most of his body covered with third-degree burns. In a haze of pain and disorientation in the ambulance, he had realized the thieves had caught both him and the dragon off guard and smothered his protective web with a blanket of agony.

He had recovered to a degree only after nine long months of hospitalization, skin grafts, and intensive therapy. His wonderful tattoos had been badly disfigured by burn scars, his friend's masterwork practically destroyed. Perhaps most heavily scarred was the Ugly Man's soul. He'd eventually ended up in the 'loin, living in a cardboard tent and spending most of his monthly SSI on "medicine" from Wild Bill's. Avoiding all unnecessary human contact, he had become fearful and paranoid, just another one of the nameless, forgotten derelicts shuffling the streets. He had remained convinced, in his few lucid moments, that the fiery scarring was undoubtedly a kind of retribution for abandoning his friend in the flaming car wreck. The accident had ended his attempt to live the Seven Virtues.

In the late morning, the Ugly Man awakened with a start. Something was noticeably different. Sucking in a deep breath to clear his head, he realized he wasn't covered with sweat. No, and his skin wasn't hurting either. He felt okay. The best he'd felt in years. His hands weren't shaking, and he didn't feel sick to his stomach at all. He held up his arm and examined his skin. Amazingly, the scars were almost completely gone. The tattoos were becoming brilliantly alive again.

Early that evening, he walked down O'Farrell with a little spring in his step. He still didn't have the shakes, despite the fact that he'd had nothing to drink all day. He'd even risked the proximity of others by eating over at St. Anthony's—put away the whole meal and didn't get sick. Once he had picked up his SSI check and cashed it over on Haight, he even hesitated to retrace his steps to Wild Bill's.

Eventually he decided to buy a half pint for backup, just in case he needed something later. He often awoke in the early morning hours, badly needing another drink even after his nightly pint. He headed for Wild Bill's.

A block from the liquor store, he stopped, spotting a pair of mean-spirited drug dealers attacking a skinny young guy. Big Foot, a heavyset huge man wearing a Raiders black pullover with the silver number 77, and his thinly built, equally creepy sidekick, Sleepyboy. The two thugs were pummeling their victim with lengths of bicycle chain, pounding him unmercifully right in the mouth of a nearby alley, completely visible to passing traffic.

"Ya gonna come up wif da bread now, white boy?" Big Foot growled. He was almost out of breath, but continued his flailing exertions.

For a moment, the Ugly Man just stood rooted to the spot and watched, wincing with each delivered blow until Sleepyboy took out a large can of lighter fluid and a cigarette lighter and aimed the makeshift flamethrower at the hapless, battered victim. With a newfound surge of courage, the Ugly Man stepped into the alley and shoved Big Foot from behind. "No," he rasped, stepping closer to Sleepyboy and slapping the can from his hand.

Big Foot turned to face him, amazed anger written all over the dope dealer's pudgy features. "Hey, hey, whatcha doin', muthahfuckah?" the huge man sputtered. "You buttin' into our bidness?" He lashed out viciously with his piece of bicycle chain. The Ugly Man ducked nimbly. The chain just grazed the top of his hood as the bludgeoned victim scrambled up to his feet and darted past him out to freedom.

"Lemme light the ole fool up, Biggie," Sleepyboy said, picking up the lighter fluid and flicking the cigarette lighter. "Fix his burnt-up ole raggedy ass for good."

The Ugly Man backed away, staring at the lighter flame fearfully, questioning the wisdom of his impulsive act.

"Yo, go 'head, torch him, Sleeps," Big Foot ordered.

The Ugly Man spun around and fled quickly up the street

before Sleepyboy could spray him with fire. Ignoring the ache in his lower right leg, he ran almost as fast as he had when he'd been a young man playing soccer, dodging skillfully in and out of the crowd, reaching his block in less than a minute and a half. Pausing to catch his breath, the Ugly Man glanced back. He could see neither of the dope dealers in pursuit, but he knew they'd be coming for him soon. No question about that.

At that moment he saw a ball bounce out into the busy street, and from the corner of his eye, he saw a youngster dart into the street after the ball.

"No!" he cried out hoarsely. Time seemed to slow as several thoughts rushed through his head: *You can't get involved here; they are coming; they will probably kill you.*

He ignored the cautionary thoughts. With long strides, the Ugly Man bounded into the street, deftly dodged a vehicle and scooped up the child and ball. He spun 180 degrees as adroitly as Reggie Bush, holding out his hand and stiff-arming a taxi to a brake-squealing stop, before finally handing off the crying child to his mother, who was still standing frozen in the doorway to the You-Do-It laundromat.

"Hey, yo, dude, way to go, man!" said Double S, a legless black man who roamed the Tenderloin on a scooterboard. He stretched up and offered the Ugly Man a high five.

The Ugly Man slapped Double S's hand, then nervously looked back down O'Farrell, remembering the threat of the two drug dealers. Still not in sight. He let a sigh trickle across his lips and glanced again at the grateful mother and her child. She held her boy tightly in her arms, talking to two female friends, gesturing at him and nodding.

Waving back, he smiled with pride and moved along for a few steps, but for some reason he stopped and shifted his gaze overhead. The nightly mist had thinned, and here and there bluish-crystal stars glistened against the black backdrop of space. It was an unusual sight this time of year; the fog usually shrouded the night sky from view. For a moment, the break in the fog and rare sight took his breath away, providing ice for his bruised soul. Momentarily, the smells, the sights, the sounds, and all the nastiness of the 'loin were gone. A sense of gratitude for just being alive overwhelmed him—something he hadn't felt for a long, long time.

With a slight shudder, thoughts of the two thugs again flooded his thoughts. The Ugly Man shuffled along quickly down his alley, past his cardboard tent to the very end. There, he squeezed in to hide behind the dumpster and collect himself.

He expected to hear footsteps any minute. He knew he should be paralyzed, but after searching his feelings and thoughts, he detected little sense of fear in himself. No, he wasn't scared at all. His fear had been replaced with...something else. In fact, he had only positive thoughts and feelings, partly because of the series of events of the past ten minutes or so, concluding with his discovery of the extraordinary star-filled night. But he was also acutely aware of the itchy, dry skin cracking along his arms and legs as he slumped down behind the dumpster. Another weird feeling, too, centered on his back—the just-noticeable sensation of something crawling. Giddy, he knew the remarkable change, whatever it signaled, was nearing completion. And he also knew that the transformation wasn't just physical; no indeed, he was dramatically changing inside, too, growing stronger. A really positive feeling about himself.

At that moment, The Ugly Man drifted; for a second or two he could almost hear his friend's mystical advice from long ago: *Follow the Way.*

Blinking, he sucked in a deep breath and looked about his cramped enclosure, assessing his immediate situation. He realized that if Big Foot and Sleepyboy tracked him back there, he would be trapped in a dead-end alley. But, then again, so would they. The thought almost made him giggle, but he restrained himself, cocked his head, and listened intently, lurking like a shadow in the night.

Another minute or so dragged by.

Overhead, the mist had thickened, again blotting out the stars.

Then came the sound of footsteps in the alleyway, cautiously approaching.

Closer.

The Ugly Man completely shed the last of his ugliness.

Transformed, he gazed back down on the alley as Big Foot and Sleepyboy paused at the cardboard tent and peeked in.

The big man angrily kicked over the dwelling place, scattering things. "Ugly dude done gone!" he said, his mean features scrunched into a dark scowl. Sleepyboy tapped the big man's shoulder and pointed to the nearby dumpster, his face deadpan.

Big Foot grinned and shuffled forward. He cautiously looked behind the dumpster and swore under his breath. "Oh, *shit*! Looky here, Sleeps."

The thinly built sidekick peered around the wide leader.

In back of the dumpster, there was only a pile of smelly clothes and a threadbare hooded sweatshirt resting atop the wrinkled shirts and pants.

With a puzzled expression, Big Foot leaned over and flicked through the pile of clothes, finally exposing what looked like a pile of discarded, cracked, marked skin, like something a huge diamondback rattler might have shed.

"What the fuck—?"

He found a stick and used it to lift up some of his discovery to show his cohort.

Revealing little emotion, Sleepyboy nodded. "The ugly ole fool done shed all his ruined skin, man. That's it right there."

Amazed, Big Foot discarded the shed skin on the pile of clothes. He shook his head, his face even more puzzled. "Fuck him, Sleeps. Let's find the skinny-ass deadbeat, an' slice his apple." He slipped something from his pocket, flicking it back and forth in the air threateningly.

The dim light glinted off the blade of the straight razor.

Sleepyboy nodded his head and began to turn away. "'Kay. Let's do him."

Overhead, the Ugly Man thought, *No, they aren't doing anyone.* He fanned his wings.

The two drug dealers froze in place, noticing the air whirling down and stirring the alley debris into a hurricane about them. Startled, they looked up at the rooftop of the two-story building at the end of the alley. He was poised on the lip of the overhang, his fearsome red gaze glaring down at them, paralyzing both in place.

Before either hoodlum could even twitch a muscle to run, he sprang off the building with an ear-shattering roar, swooped down, and engulfed both men in a blistering inferno that lit up the cool night.

BALANCE

At 6:55 a.m., when Declan Mulcahy first stepped out onto O'Farrell Street from his apartment building, San Francisco's Tenderloin district appeared sunny and warm but uncharacteristically deserted—a brief lull between changing shifts. Most of the dealers, junkies, and hookers had called it a night; the homeless were still asleep in their cardboard tents, and the neighborhood street cops were all up at Happy Donuts doing police work.

Declan walked a block up the street from his apartment and met only an old Asian lady coming from the opposite direction. She pulled a little red wagon stacked with two baskets of dirty clothes, obviously headed for the nearby You Do It laundromat. He crossed the street and saw one other person, a black dude waiting for the Korean's grocery store to open. The guy was about Declan's age, late twenties to early thirties, sporting dreadlocks and frayed camouflage utilities—no name tag or unit designation, only the faded Army patch remained intact over his heart. Declan had seen him around in the past month or so, often leaving the Korean's with a small brown sack. Sometimes he wondered if the guy had been in Desert Storm, too. But he never asked, only nodded.

Declan was wound pretty tight that morning. He'd been up most of the night, his mouth almost too dry to ask anything, his underarms and crotch gritty and damp with clammy sweat. He sniffed, reminded that sweat smelled different, depending on the type. Work sweat had kind of a neutral odor, mildly offensive at worst; sex sweat lingered on you, smelled good, especially when mixed with traces of perfume; booze or dope sweat the morning after had a stale, nauseating smell; but the absolute worst smell of all was nervous fear sweat—sharp, sour, and biting. At that moment the sharp stink was flaring his nostrils, making them itch.

He rubbed his nose, sucked in a deep breath, closed his eyes, and centered for a moment to settle his nerves. Then, at 7:00 sharp, Declan followed the guy in Army cams into the store.

Mr. Pak himself had opened the front door and stepped back

behind the service counter. He bowed politely to his two early morning customers in his self-deprecating way, an old-world mannerism that neither of his teenaged children practiced. Both had grown up on the mean streets of the 'loin, attending local public schools. Declan nodded back, wandered over to the video machine, and waited impatiently for the black dude to pick out his Old English forty-ouncer from the drink box, pay, and get the fuck out of the grocery. Then it would be only Mr. Pak, alone in the store, and his two kids either in back where goods were stored or in the family flat upstairs getting ready for high school.

Declan slipped to the back of the store and took a quick peek through the round window in the swinging door leading to the storage area. The boy was back there, occupied with cutting open cases of various canned items. Declan tilted his head, listened intently, and could just make out the girl moving around upstairs. The entire family was on the premises and accounted for at this early hour, just as planned. Yes, indeed.

After the dude in the Army cams carefully counted his change twice and finally left the store with his brown bag, Declan stepped up to the counter.

The middle-aged Korean grocer looked at him curiously. "You no find something?"

Declan shook his head, closed his eyes, and concentrated. *Mr. Pak, you know the reason I am here, right?* he thought. Then he blinked, steeled himself, reached under his dark green USF sweatshirt, and slipped the recently purchased Colt Python .357 out of the front of his Levi's.

At first Mr. Pak nodded and smiled, as if answering Declan's silent question; then the smile froze on his face and his eyes widened when he spotted the gun. Both hands flew up in a defensive gesture as he said in a shaky voice, "You no stealy-boy. Why you do this?"

Declan didn't answer as time, movement, and his thinking seemed to alter dramatically into super-slow motion. On a kind of pre-programmed autopilot, he gently squeezed the handgun's trigger.

The gunshot made a sharp, high-pitched whine, characteristic of a .357, shattering the stillness in the store. The sound made Declan's eardrums vibrate painfully. He hadn't anticipated this trait of the gun and had neglected to use cotton earplugs. He ground his teeth against the pain.

The grocer tumbled backward into the wall behind the check-out counter, a crimson flower slowly appearing over his right eye as he finally slid inelegantly to the floor.

"Papa...Papa!" a voice screamed to Declan's far left. The teenage daughter stood frozen on the bottom step of the staircase leading to the family flat. She held her hands up to either side of her round face as if holding her head on her shoulders. A shocked, disbelieving expression glazed her dark eyes.

Swinging his gun hand slowly around in her direction, Declan squeezed the .357's trigger again; the round hit the young woman in the chest.

Unlike her father, she fell forward, face down, after her right leg buckled and slipped off the last step. Declan watched as a thick pool of blood spread out from her upper body.

For a brief moment, he closed his eyes, feeling time and place slipping away from his mental grasp, like so many other times in the past few years. He felt himself pulled back to the Storm, the night his Force Recon unit was surprised, almost wiped out under a thundering barrage of friendly rocket fire.

"No," Declan whispered hoarsely, blinking and resisting the pull of the past. He did not need to relive the pyrotechnic horror show again.

Turning his back on the fallen father and daughter, Declan glimpsed a frightened face in the round window of the door at the rear of the store. Still moving in slow motion, he took five giant steps down the nearest aisle and pushed the storage room door open with his free hand, pointing inside with the Colt.

The boy tried to escape, bounding slowly up and down, heading for a rear exit into the alley behind the store. Declan's third shot hit him in the lower back, sprawling the teenager forward onto all fours, a red stain spreading across the back of his white T-shirt. Legs useless, the boy struggled for a moment or two toward the alley exit, pulling himself along the floor with his arms in an awkward swimming motion. Making little progress, he looked back over his shoulder, his face a grimace of pain, and said something. It appeared like lip-synching, because by then Declan was completely deafened by the three high-pitched blasts. He moved alongside the boy, leaned down, and gently pressed the weapon to the back of the young boy's head. He fired a fourth time, ending the teenager's agony.

The operation was over, mission completed. Probably less than two minutes. Declan slipped the weapon back into the front of his Levi's.

Weak-kneed and shaking slightly, he managed to make it to a sink in the corner of the storeroom. He expected to throw up, like after the slaughter of his unit during the Storm, but he was only slightly nauseated. He used his finger and gagged forcefully twice, managing only to make his eyes water heavily. He should feel some remorse for the Pak family, who had always been polite and helpful. Kind, even. *No,* he chastised himself, *you can't think like that.* They had all three been volunteers, helping counteract the Law of Catastrophic Isostasy.

Sometime shortly after the last shot, Declan's thinking and perception had sped back up to real time. He wiped his eyes with the back of his hand, took a deep breath, and washed his face with cool water. As he straightened up from the sink, the ringing in his ears began to subside.

Declan pushed the swinging door back into the store, about the same time a neighborhood bag lady shuffled in the front door and looked around, frowning angrily. "Say, boy, where's that ole Gung Ho or one of 'em young'ns? I needs a coffee, bad."

Declan shrugged, turning his face down and away as he pushed by the impatient old woman on the way to the street, mumbling, "Dunno."

He crossed O'Farrell, looked anxiously back over his shoulder once, and realized no one was following. He hurried down the block back to his building, the street still relatively empty of pedestrians and traffic. Everything had gone real smooth, according to plan. Yes, indeed.

* * *

Inside his studio apartment, Declan glanced around cautiously. The tiny room, sparsely furnished, appeared undisturbed. He stepped over to the chipped desk his social worker had given him and re-aligned the three pencils parallel with the edge of his writing pad. Yes, everything was neat and simple, just like his room had been at the VA hospital in Martinez. Except there he'd had to go into the dayroom to see TV. Here in his apartment, Declan sat down on his one folding chair and stared at the portable black and white set with its rabbit ears. But he didn't turn on the TV, just stared intently at the blank grey screen and waited patiently, a skill he'd developed over the years during his stays at Martinez.

After a few minutes, a figure materialized on the screen: a woman, looking just like the blindfolded statue down at the Hall of Justice. Only the scales held by the TV Lady Justice were balanced evenly.

Declan sighed deeply with relief.

At that moment, a feminine voice in his head announced: *You did very well, Declan Mulcahy. Very well indeed, considering it was your first assignment. I am quite impressed by your effective and timely performance. But, to validate to yourself that we have indeed counteracted the Law of Catastrophic Isostasy, please peruse the San Francisco Chronicle tomorrow morning, noting the complete absence of any reported disasters.*

Declan nodded and smiled as Lady Justice faded from the blank screen. *Yes,* he promised himself, *I will definitely check the newspaper tomorrow.*

Early the next morning, Declan walked up O'Farrell, glancing nervously across the street as he passed the Korean's grocery. SFPD yellow crime scene tape roped it off, and quite a few cops were still on the scene, talking to pedestrians up and down both sides of the street. A TV van from Channel 7 was set up nearby, too. It looked like that Melendez lady talking into the camera. None of the policemen seemed the least bit interested in stopping Declan or asking him questions. Apparently they hadn't interviewed the bag lady, or maybe she hadn't been able to ID him. Either way, he breathed more easily and walked quickly past the cops.

Declan continued two blocks up to the corner of Jones and crossed over to Homeboy's liquor store to buy a Chronicle.

Back out on the street, Declan anxiously thumbed through the newspaper. No Oklahoma City bombings, no hurricanes, no earthquakes, no tornados, no floods, not even a thunderstorm reported in the Midwest. His held breath trickled out across his dry lips. The voice in his head, the Lady Justice, had been right. The intervention had definitely worked; they had managed to keep the scales balanced.

Jacked up by the results of the successful covert operation, Declan turned to head back home, grinning at the dude in the Army cams who was apparently coming in to get his morning taste of Old English up at Homeboy's now that the Korean was out of business.

The guy nodded and spoke as he passed Declan. "Whassup?"

Declan didn't answer, surprised by the first verbal greeting in a month or so of exchanging nods. He strolled on back down O'Farrell, the Chronicle tucked under his arm.

Back in his tiny apartment, Declan went through the newspaper, page by page, more carefully, making sure he hadn't missed something. He'd been right the first time; no disasters, man-made or natural, reported anywhere across the country. He smiled to himself, feeling pretty good.

Actually, really good.

The best he'd felt since leaving the hospital four weeks before. Yes, indeed.

After returning home to San Francisco from the Gulf and Desert Storm, Declan had spent eight years going in and out of the North Bay VA hospital a dozen times. The surgeons had done a pretty good job on his bad leg—he had only a slight limp—but the doctors had ended up with less luck with his damaged psyche, or so they claimed. Over that time, the psychiatrists and clinical psychologists at the hospital had built up an impressive ten-inch file of extensive test results, observational anecdotes, and diagnoses. Most of the technical jargon was incomprehensible to Declan, with the exception of post-traumatic stress disorder and the two words often tacked on at the end of a diagnostic rambling: delusion and hallucination. He suspected that most of the psychiatric babble was inaccurate, especially the treatment prescriptions, because each time he returned to San Francisco from Martinez—even when he attended outpatient therapy two to three times a week at the VA center and took his meds faithfully every day—he *still* couldn't hold a regular job, attend City College for even a short summer session, or maintain a relationship with a regular woman. In fact, nothing seemed to work out right no matter how hard Declan tried. After all these years, he'd finally decided that the nightmare night during the Storm had done nothing to his head; instead, it had permanently damaged his soul. Who could cure that?

So repeatedly, soon after each return to city life from the hospital, he gave up and just drifted, living off his disability checks, drinking and taking street drugs at the first of the month when he still had cash, occasionally being arrested. His social worker was usually able to talk the judge out of sending him to jail by promising to send Declan back to the psychiatric ward at the VA hospital. Most of the past eight years had been a monotonous blur.

But after Declan's most recent release from the hospital, life had finally improved. He'd moved into his new apartment, stopped going to outpatient care at the VA center, and quit taking the mind-numbing meds. The only minor bump had been when Declan's social worker, Ms. Latisha, had come by one night the week before and hassled him about not going to outpatient at Clement. She'd also bugged him about religiously taking all his prescribed medication and staying off the dope and booze.

"You will freak out again, hear and see shit not really there..." Yakety yakety yak.

She threatened to send him back to the hospital if he didn't conform. Of course he didn't tell her he wasn't taking any of the damned pills. He just nodded and replied agreeably half a dozen times at appropriate moments during the harangue, "Yes, I will, Ms. L." or, "You are absolutely right, Ms. L."

After she finally left, Declan sat in the folding chair and

stared at the blank TV, feeling a little bummed out by her threats but knowing that, despite her warnings, his thinking was the sharpest it had been since the Storm. No hallucinations, no freaking out. Everything cool. Yes, indeed.

A few minutes after declaring himself perfectly stable, Declan saw something strange materialize on the grey TV screen. A figure: Lady Justice. She appeared just like she did down at the Hall of Justice on Bryant: all in white, blindfolded, holding tipped scales. Really beautiful. For several moments he just stared, admiring her. Then, even though the statue's lips did not move, Declan heard a female voice in his head—not shrill and harping like Ms. L, but gentle and kind—and he knew it was the Lady Justice speaking to him.

Declan Mulcahy, your country needs your services again. A top secret covert military operation. Do you understand?

He nodded, then shut his eyes and concentrated, thinking: *Yes, I understand you. What kind of operation?*

You will be a part of a special unit, each person operating independently, counteracting the Law of Catastrophic Isostasy—

The law of what? he interrupted.

Catastrophic Isostasy, Lady Justice repeated. *You see, every time there is a major natural or man-made catastrophe somewhere in the world—floods, typhoons, earthquakes, volcanic eruptions, bombings, that type of thing—there will be a corresponding disaster of equal magnitude occurring in this country. A kind of global balancing of violence.*

She paused at that point, allowing him a moment to process and understand the impact of the law.

Unless, she continued, her voice rising slightly in pitch and volume, *unless we intervene with a relatively minor amount of counterbalancing force. This is your job, a direct intervention preventing application of the Law of Catastrophic Isostasy. Do you understand?*

I—I am not sure, Declan thought.

It's like homeostasis, the elements of the human body always tending to maintain a stable state of equilibrium. A question of balance. You remember that from biology in school?

Yes, I think so.

The Earth is just another organism maintaining a homeostatic balance among various elements, one action requiring a global counteraction: the Law of Catastrophic Isostasy. But if we intervene, react with a certain minimal level of effective force, then we can cancel out a much more devastating national disaster.

It was getting clearer, making more sense. *I see. But exactly what will we be doing to stop these terrible events from happening?*

We watch, Declan. TV newscasts like CNN; read the newspaper. We do everything possible to keep current on catastrophes as they occur in other parts of the world. Then... She paused again, continuing a moment later in a more business-like tone, *Then we search locally, identify and terminate elements that originated in that other part of the world.*

Elements? Declan thought.

Yes. For example, after an earthquake disaster in Japan, we must immediately eliminate a number of Japanese-Americans. Or after a flood on the Ivory Coast, a number of African-Americans will need to be sacrificed.

You mean we must assassinate someone here to prevent a bigger natural disaster?

Yes, but we use only volunteers. I recruit each of them prior to your visit.

It was all clear now. Counteracting the Law of Catastrophic Isostasy made perfect sense to Declan. He would be balancing justice's scales. He felt a surge of excitement. He would be doing something valuable, contributing to his country's welfare. Like what he'd been trained to do in the Marines.

This is all highly secret, Declan Mulcahy. Discuss this with no one, especially your social worker.

No, I understand, Declan thought. *She gets only name, rank, serial number, and date of birth.*

Lady Justice actually chuckled.

Several nights later, on the channel two 10:00 p.m. news, Declan saw the announcement of the typhoon sweeping across the East China Sea, devastating a tiny village on the coast southwest of Pusan, Korea. Over a hundred casualties. After he turned off the TV, he was visited by Lady Justice on the blank screen, who gave him his first assignment: the termination of all three members of the Pak family.

* * *

A week after the successful operation at the Korean grocery, Declan watched the tail end of a CNN broadcast on a big screen at The Good Guys on Geary Street. A small village in the Chilean Andes had been almost totally destroyed that morning by a volcanic eruption; one hundred and twenty-five villagers were missing or identified as dead. He watched for a few more minutes, recognizing the potential hazard to his country—Catastrophic Isostasy would soon be kicking in, if something were not done quickly.

Declan hurried to the closest Muni stop and caught a bus for home.

Inside his apartment in the heart of the 'loin, he took his seat and waited, staring at the blank TV screen. He didn't have to wait long, only a few minutes, before Lady Justice appeared.

Ah, Declan, you know about the village in the Andes?

Yes.

This time, your operation involves only one target. Edwina Sanchez, a recent illegal immigrant from Chile, a man who dresses like a woman and works the sex trade in the Tenderloin. He is very tall—six foot two—speaks with a heavy Spanish accent, and usually wears a blonde wig. Late in the evening, Edwina solicits business in front of the Majestic Arms Hotel around the corner on Jones. You must complete the operation tonight. Is all that clear?

Yes, it is, Declan thought, nodding.

Your acquaintance on the scooterboard will be able to help locate Edwina Sanchez.

Declan knew she was referring to his friend Short Stuff, a double-leg amputee Marine vet of Vietnam, now a street hustler who knew everything that happened in the 'loin.

As it got dark, traffic increased on Jones Street. Some cars slowed as they moved by the Majestic and a chilling fog clung to the dirty brick facade of the once grand hotel where many of the ground-floor rooms were now available for a $5-hourly rate.

When Declan first walked up, Sweet Jane hit on him, all tricked out in her low-cut red blouse, black vinyl miniskirt, and red high heels. She grabbed him possessively, rubbing her breasts against his arm and licking her glossy lips suggestively. "Hey, man, you ready to party or what?" the redhead asked, her heavy perfume flaring Declan's nostrils.

He shook his head but smiled. "Can't tonight, Sweet Jane. Looking for Edwina?"

"Tall tranny, speaks funny?"

He nodded.

"Hey, man, whatcha want with that fake shit?" she asked, reaching down with one hand and making a lewd grabbing gesture at her own crotch. "You know you got the real thing right here."

"Nah, it ain't like that," he explained, embarrassed by her implication. "This ain't actually a partying deal. He owes a friend some money."

Sweet Jane smiled and winked. "Okay, man, see you later then?"

"We'll see," he said, not explaining that he'd given up all forms of partying. No drugs, booze, or women since he'd first been visited by Lady Justice.

The redhead moved away, exaggerating her hip swing for Declan's benefit. He watched her walk half a block, then wave at an emerald green Mercury Topaz that braked and pulled over to the curb. A moment or two of negotiation, then Sweet Jane hopped into the front seat of the car. She'd caught a live one.

Around 11:00 p.m., Declan spotted his amputee friend pushing his way on his scooterboard along the sidewalk.

"Yo," Declan said, offering his fist.

"'Sup, Irish?" Double S said, lightly punching Declan's knuckles.

"Just kicking here at the hotel, watching for Edwina," Declan said, trying to sound casual. "You know the dude? He owes my friend money."

"Yep, jus' seen him workin' traffic 'round the corner by Homeboy's 'bout ten minutes ago," Double S answered, firing up a smoke.

"All right, bro, buy yourself a taste," Declan said. He tapped Double S's fist again and slipped him a couple of bucks before limping off for the liquor store around the corner.

Declan lured Edwina down an alley half a block up from Homeboy's with a $20 bill paid in advance for quick sex. As the tall transvestite kneeled on a piece of cardboard in the darkened alley, Declan carefully slipped his Colt from the back of his Levi's and aimed the handgun down at Edwina's blonde wig. *Time for Lady Justice to be served, man*, he thought as movement and perception shifted down into super slow-motion.

As if privy to the thought, the Chilean glanced up from unzipping Declan's jeans with a frightened expression, just a long moment before the trigger squeeze and the sharp crack of the .357.

This time Declan had inserted two pieces of cotton into his ears. Protected from the deafening crack of the weapon, he watched the kneeling man slump forward at his feet. Slowly, he moved back to a dumpster, selected a sheet of cardboard, and covered the skimpily-dressed transvestite. Again, he felt little emotion. He realized that Edwina Sanchez had been terminated as one unit, a small part of a larger plan—a self-sacrificing volunteer.

Time, perception, and movement all quickly returned to normal as Declan slipped away from the dead body. He paused at the mouth of the alley to ensure bypassers had not heard the shot. No one paid him any attention as he left the alley and headed for his apartment.

The figure materialized on the grey screen, her scales perfectly balanced.

Declan was jumpy the next evening, worrying the police would come by. He didn't want them picking him up and interrupting his participation in Lady Justice's secret operation. *Not now*, he prayed silently. *I am finally doing something worthwhile, something good.* Yes, indeed.

At 9:00 p.m. he went out to walk off his unease.

It was Friday night and the 'loin was rocking. The sidewalks were crowded with people shouting, laughing, buying and selling; music blared from the bars and second story open windows along the street. Cars squealed, braking and honking. Buses deposited clouds of diesel fumes over it all. Noisy, sweaty, smelly.

Declan wandered for a few minutes, ending up at the alley near Homeboy's, surprised there was no crime scene yellow tape around the site. He glanced down the alley; the cardboard shroud was gone, the body of the dead transvestite obviously removed. Apparently no big deal, no big loss…almost like it hadn't really happened.

The last thought struck a negative chord.

Declan could hear Ms. L.'s admonition about taking his meds very clearly over the street hubbub: *You will freak out again, hear and see shit that isn't really there.*

Jesus, was he just freaking out again?

Maybe the whole thing was just in his head—seeing Lady Justice on his blank TV, the Law of Catastrophic Isostasy, the whole special operation. Summarized simply like that, it did sound kind of crazy.

Could that be?

For a moment, Declan was confused. Then he recovered his poise and told himself emphatically, "No, Ms. L. is wrong!"

Declan was one hundred percent sure he'd scored the Colt from a street hustler, Big Henry, the previous week over on Turk Street. He was positive that a week ago he'd really terminated the Pak family. Last night he'd shot Edwina, too.

"Whassup, man?"

The dude in the Army cams had come out of Homeboy's with his brown bag and slipped up quietly enough to startle Declan.

"You a Marine?" the guy asked, gesturing toward the faded USMC patch on Declan's field jacket.

"Yeah, I was once."

"You do the Gulf and the Storm?"

Declan nodded.

"What unit?"

"Force Recon."

"Heavy," the guy said, as if approving the answer. "I did the Storm, too, but as regular Army infantry. Buy you a drink?" He held up the brown bag and gestured toward the alley.

Declan hesitated a second—he'd drunk no alcohol since becoming part of the secret operation. *Why not?*

"Sure."

He followed the Storm vet a few steps into the darkness. The dude slipped the brown paper bag down off his bottle, unscrewed the top off the half-empty forty-ouncer, then wiped the mouth clean before he handed it over to Declan.

Declan nodded, accepted the bag, and took a long pull on the Old English malt liquor. It was cold and sharp. Wiping his mouth, he said, "Hey thanks, man, that hit the spot," and handed the bagged forty-ouncer back.

That's when Declan saw it.

The guy was pointing a .45 automatic, military issue, at his chest.

Lady ordered up your raggedy ass, man. You prob'ly didn't see the bombing on the news from Belfast?

Pulse racing, Declan just shook his head numbly.

I.R.A. action last night at a pub in the downtown protestant section. Bomb wasted three, including a member of parliament, and wounded another dozen. No telling how many'll get whacked during payback.

Declan opened his mouth to speak aloud and complain that the Lady hadn't contacted him. He wasn't a volunteer for this end of the operation, even though he was indeed Irish-American. Was this how his role in the operation ended, so suddenly? His last contribution to the cause a self-sacrifice? He smiled wryly and nodded acceptance, closing his mouth without speaking. After all, who was he really? An unemployed, scruffy, disabled vet—probably even mentally ill, like the shrinks all agreed. He was indeed insignificant. Even so, he was still a small cog in a much greater mechanism.

The .45 flashed in the darkness.

Declan never heard the shot.

Despite his gritty resignation to a grim fate, Declan didn't die instantly in that alley. The .45 round hit him in the chest, breaking a pair of ribs, puncturing a lung, tearing a saucer-sized exit wound in his back, but remarkably missing his heart and all other vital organs. Three hours after being shot, Declan still clung to life, in critical condition, on full support in the trauma ward at San Francisco General Hospital.

Alive, but unconscious and completely unaware of the 6.4 earthquake that rattled the city that morning at 12:25 a.m.

THE APOTHEOSIS
OF NATHAN MCKEE

Jelly Doughnuts

Nathan McKee sat completely naked, except for his taped ribs, on the foot of his bed in his drab room in the Hotel Reo. Tiny beads of sweat popped out on his pale body, forehead, and upper lip as he waited with a rising sense of nervous anticipation. He wondered if the altered state would hit him again that evening—a rare emotional and speculative state of mind.

Nathan hadn't felt or thought much of anything since his wife, Geri, and their son, Davy, had died in an automobile accident near Kezar Stadium ten years before. For most of the past decade he'd aimlessly wandered the Tenderloin district of San Francisco in a numbed daze, his sensibilities usually anesthetized by liberal dozes of Old English, Gallo Tokay, and Wild Irish Rose. Once a hard-charging tailored suit on Montgomery Street in the financial district, he'd squandered everything since the accident, lucky now to even own a threadbare, greasy navy blue topcoat. If it weren't for the monthly SSI checks, he would have been sleeping in a cardboard tent in an alley. As it was, Nathan always found himself panhandling at the end of each month just to make ends meet—a fifty-year-old drunken bum.

He'd been booze-free for an entire week, ever since he'd been badly beaten and experienced a grand mal seizure over on O'Farrell Street near Homeboy's on Friday. The ass-kicking had resulted in a heavily medicated four-day stay in San Francisco General. Yes, indeed, still clean and sober after being back on the street unsupervised for three days—in-*fucking*-credible.

Nathan waited, relishing his accelerated pulse rate, the slight adrenaline rush, and his heightened sensibility. He gazed with interest out the sixth story dirty window that faced westerly over Jones Street, watching the sun as it began to drop out of sight behind the buildings along Van Ness hill, streaking the clouded sky with neon oranges and violets.

He knew he didn't have long to wait.

As dusk settled over the 'loin, Nathan again experienced the familiar onset of the anticipated seizure, exactly like the two nights since being released from SF Gen: a sudden, painful tightening of the muscles in the pit of his stomach that doubled him over, followed immediately by a rapid increase in his heart rate. A moment later, an apparent forty-degree drop in the room temperature chilled his sweaty body, making him clench his teeth. He groaned, upright but partially paralyzed, his breathing labored. His vision tunneled, and Nathan slipped into that other place…

Disoriented, dizzy, nauseated…surroundings surreal, deep in a cold, dark cavern. Drawn toward blinding lights, then stopping suddenly…like standing in the dark backstage of an empty theatre and peering into glaring floodlights, frozen like a deer caught in the headlights of an onrushing car.

Abruptly, the stage curtain began to silently lower, dropping ever so slowly, gradually blocking out even the tiniest glimmer of light. Total blackness, like a starless night fallen in on itself. Alone in the dark. After a few moments, he felt the sensation of sinking, as if he were being sucked down a black drain.

Consciousness slipping…

Nathan awoke, still sitting completely nude on the foot of his bed. In the fifteen or so minutes he'd been unconscious, night had begun to settle heavily over the city, cloaking his room in darkness.

Taking a quick personal inventory, he felt pretty good—his breath, vision, and pulse rate were all back to normal, and his skin temperature had warmed up considerably. But, like the past two nights, his deathly pale body and limbs had been altered during the seizure, taking on an inky mottling with a peculiar 3-D blurring effect. Staring into the palm of his hand was like looking into a deep black pool of water that absorbed all light, reflecting nothing back; his hand and fingers became indistinct. Even close up, only a foot or so from his face, his hand looked blurry. After stretching his arm out, the hand and wrist disappeared completely, blending in perfectly with the room's increasing darkness. Nervously, Nathan flexed his lower legs and toes and fingered the clear tape just under his right armpit, still tightly binding the two cracked ribs. With a dry chuckle, he concluded, "Guess I'm still in one piece." It never occurred to him to call the doctors about his nightly skin alteration. Over the years he'd learned to accept whatever the Tenderloin dealt him with fatalistic resignation.

Nathan stood up, but stumbled and had to reach out to steady himself for a few seconds against the wall, his legs drained of energy, unsteady. He took a deep breath, then stepped cautiously across the small room, pausing for a second and glancing with boyish glee into the cracked dresser mirror a yard or two away. He saw an empty, unlit room, and only a slight distortion of the dark atmosphere where he stood, as if a slight breeze had disturbed a wave of heat rising from a floor vent.

Dismissing any attempted explanations of the remarkable transformation, Nathan chuckled loudly as he left the room, still unclothed.

At the foot of the stairs leading into the dingy hotel lobby, Nathan paused and glanced left at Ferdie, who did not even look up from the barred window at the front desk. The night clerk was busy laying out keys for the first floor rooms, most of which rented for hourly rates. That night, Friday, would be hectic, a constant stream of women and their customers coming in from the street. Nathan wondered why Ferdie bothered with the keys at all. Half of the door locks in the old, run-down Reo—especially those on the busy first floor—didn't work.

He shrugged and deftly dodged to the side to avoid being run over by an eager couple hurrying in the opened doors of the hotel. The hooker led a red-faced, fat john to the front desk, where the john dug out and handed Ferdie a five-dollar bill and received a key in return. The numbered keys did benefit the night clerk, in a way; they helped Ferdie keep track of which rooms were in use.

Satisfied that neither the couple nor Ferdie could see him, Nathan turned from the front desk and stepped outside, shivering in the cool evening air and glancing about.

Early Friday night and the Tenderloin was already rockin'-n-rollin'. Jones Street traffic was stalled-out bumper-to-bumper waiting for the lights to change over on Geary. Horns blasted, people shouted, Muni buses belched out diesel fumes, and the sidewalk was already littered with trash and crowded with a representative sample of the city's underclass—recent immigrants, furtive sellers of hot goods and special services, and even a pair of young children joyfully playing tag in and out of the adults in addition to the usual desolate and desperate human beings. A kind of nervous energy electrified the atmosphere, giving it the Midwest tingle of a hovering thunderstorm. The 'loin was loud, smelly, dirty, and congested with restless excitement.

All of this sound and fury bombarded Nathan's senses as he moved along, protecting his injured ribs with his right elbow. It felt almost like something he was experiencing for the first time, which was true in a way. He had not noticed much of anything specific about the Tenderloin for a long time, with the exception of the location of several liquor stores. Not until the strange seizures and changes.

Unlike the previous two evenings of just wandering around naked like an unseen, laughing idiot, Nathan had something in mind that night, a destination and a goal. Oh, yeah. He grinned deviously to himself.

Heading north toward Geary Street, Nathan spotted Sweet Jane just ahead on the fringe of the crowd with her back against a building front—a hooker from the Reo who occasionally slipped him a buck or two at the end of the month. She was playing her violin, something she sometimes did on the street before work. Mostly classical stuff. At the moment it was "When a Gypsy Makes His Violin Cry." The majority of the mob ignored her, but a few people stopped to listen, as did Nathan, making a little island in the moving river. Sweet Jane, whom he'd probably passed by hundreds of times during the past few years without really paying close attention, played exceptionally well. Her eyes were closed and a peaceful smile rested on her pretty but lined and aging face. Nathan nodded. Another depressing story among the Tenderloin's many? Maybe, but he didn't see it that way. Listening to her play was like glimpsing a fallen angel flexing her damaged wings, trying to fly and transcend her grim circumstances.

"Gotta go to work now," Sweet Jane announced, taking the instrument from under her chin and shrugging her shoulders reluctantly at the disappointed faces of the few who had paused to listen. She bent down and put the violin in the battered case after scooping up the handful of coins inside. Obviously the woman wasn't playing for the pitiful change. Nathan shook his head.

Continuing up the street, he worked his way through the swelling crowd, enjoying his clear-headed alertness. People paid no attention to his undressed state. No one really saw Nathan at all as he shouldered his way through the delay at the stoplight.

Finally, he reached his goal: the open entry to All-Star Donuts on Post Street. He closed his eyes and savored the rich smells that assailed his nostrils. He had drunk no alcohol for seven days, his heavily medicated state in SF Gen helping him avoid any of the usual withdrawal symptoms and booze calls, but since hitting the street again he had experienced an intense craving for sugar.

Nathan opened his eyes, waited for a few moments, then strolled into the doughnut shop that he'd picked so carefully. The half of the shop to the right was completely dark; the stools, lunch counter, and tables were closed for the night. Only the pastry display counter and cash register to the left were well-lit.

The two clerks behind the cash register gossiped in their nasal, sing-song native language. Neither girl noticed the naked old man who slid to the right around the dark side of the counter, and after a moment of pondering choices, helped himself to a pair of raspberry jelly-filled doughnuts from the aluminum trays. Then Nathan backed into the dimness near the rear wall and ate both pilfered doughnuts on the spot with impunity. Each of the white-iced pastries hovered magically in the air in the long wall mirror before rapidly disappearing from sight in three or four huge bites.

Nathan licked his sticky fingers, unable to restrain a burp after eating the sweets too fast.

The nearest girl must have heard him; she turned suddenly, the frown on her face quickly dissolving into a look of puzzlement. *So much for the inscrutable countenance of the stereotypical Chinese,* Nathan thought, chuckling to himself as he left, his jones satisfied for the moment.

He wandered the rest of the evening.

Finally driven inside by the chilling fog that rolled in from the bay around midnight, Nathan waited patiently on the foot of his bed. The seizure soon hit again, the events in the other place exactly the same as earlier at dusk, only reversed in sequential order.

Unconsciousness...

Complete darkness, chilling cold, alone.

A line of light appeared at foot level, expanding as the stage curtain rose, the full glare of the floodlights blinding, everything almost dreamlike.

Sickening disorientation, dizziness...

Nathan once again sat on the foot of his bed, completely drained of energy. He glanced at the reflection in the cracked dresser mirror and nodded a sarcastic greeting.

"Glad to see you back, you pale old fart."

Then he slipped on his raggedy grey underwear and climbed under the frayed brown Army blanket, drifting off almost instantly into a deep sleep.

Incident at Homeboy's Liquor Store

The next morning, Nathan remained stretched out on his narrow bed at the Hotel Reo after he awoke. He tried to apply his once world-class analytical mind to the peculiar situation at hand. What was going on?

He seemed to be subject to a special kind of seizure he could trigger at will after dark by relaxing in the nude, and the seizure led to a remarkable skin alteration. With his transformed skin, he could walk around after dark with no one able to see him, or even aware of his presence. Truly an amazing situation.

Of course it was quite possible, Nathan admitted to himself, his elation flattening out, that he had finally gone around the corner, that the booze had gotten to him, and that he was suffering from some kind of alcohol-induced psychosis. He wasn't too different from so many others wandering the Tenderloin, talking to their invisible buddies. Just nutty old bums, except that he was a nutty old *naked* bum. But he didn't think that was really the case. People in the 'loin were pretty tolerant, but at the very least some indignant immigrant mother would have drawn the line at his full nudity in front of her kids and called the cops. Perhaps more importantly, his mind seemed different since leaving the hospital, much sharper, his thinking clear, his recall of recent events perfectly intact.

Nathan didn't think he was crazy. This alteration was real, not imaginary. Maybe an important question to consider was why he had this special ability.

"Okay," he said to himself, frowning and sitting upright. "Let's back up a week and take it from the beginning."

On Friday night, the thirtieth of June, he'd been cadging coins up on the five hundred block of O'Farrell—still part of the 'loin, but a better class of apartment residents up there, most of them employed. He'd almost managed enough panhandled money to swing a half pint of Wild Irish Rose. It would get him by until the next day, and maybe his SSI check, usually not delivered until the third, would be on time.

That was when he spotted the young white dude in a suit up at the corner near Homeboy's, glancing around nervously. A mark, if he ever saw one. Nathan hustled right up, sticking out his hand. "Say, man, can you spare some change. I ain't ate all day." A damn lie, of course. He'd eaten well over at St. Anthony's earlier that afternoon.

The guy looked startled, spooked. Then, with a frightened shake of his head, he bolted, darting around a parked Cougar that was idling in Homeboy's white zone, jumping in behind the wheel, and speeding away.

"Jesus, what hap—?" Nathan began to mumble aloud.

He was cut off, almost jerked off his feet backward.

"Fuck ya'll doin', wethead?" a voice growled menacingly from behind him.

Choked by the tightened collars of both his shirt and topcoat, Nathan managed to painfully twist his head enough to get a view of his attacker.

His heart stopped.

It was Black Angus.

The huge man loomed behind him in the mouth of an alley, his face contorted with anger.

"Yeah, you smelly ole fool," Baby Junior said as he stepped

out of the shadowed alley, moving close. Spittle splattered Nathan's chest as the thinly-built young man with a nasty fish hook scar on his cheek got right up in his face. "See what you done?" said Baby Junior in an accusatory tone. He stabbed his finger in the direction of the Cougar's departing tail lights.

Oh, man, Nathan thought, staring at the speeding car, his heart sinking. These two were crack dealers. The white guy must have been a potential customer.

As Nathan turned back to face them, his situation got drastically worse. Eug, another dealer—and one of the craziest—was standing a step or two back in the alley darkness. He casually flipped open a straight razor; the blade glinted brightly in the dim light.

Big trouble.

"Ya'll done scared off bidness, fuckhead," Black Angus said slowly, each word pronounced distinctly. His face was deadpan, his eyes colder than black ice, as he easily dragged Nathan into the alley, nearer his razor-wielding partner.

"Ole fool need his ass whupped!" Baby Junior declared, like a judge proclaiming sentence. He turned his face toward the third dealer, who was grinning back humorlessly, exposing two gold-capped front teeth and nodding in agreement.

"I hear ya, bro," Eug replied, swinging the razor at arm's length across his body as if it were a scythe. The blade was a quick, lethal blur, the dealer's eyes hooded but bright with excitement. "Lemme give him a shave afterwards."

Nathan tensed up, but caught like he was in Angus's firm grip, he couldn't possibly escape. Mesmerized, he stared first at Eug's weapon, then the man's equally evil smile.

At that moment something smashed unexpectedly into Nathan's face, knocking him backward into the alley's brick wall. He slumped down with a thud onto his butt, pain making him see pinwheels of swirling red. The hurt centered in the middle of his face; his nose was probably broken. Blinking away the flow of tears, Nathan reached up, intending to wipe away the blood that dripped from his upper lip.

A kick crashed into his exposed right armpit, expelling all the air from his lungs and causing a sharp, painful sensation between his ribs. The back of his head slammed against the bricks.

Dazed, his head and body wracked with pain, Nathan groaned loudly.

"Here's somepin else for ya nasty ole raggedy ass."

Again, Nathan's head was driven back into the brick wall by a glancing blow from a fist to his left cheek.

"Lemme cut the stinky bum, Angus—"

"Hey, you dudes, *cops* coming!" a voice warned from the street. "Let's do a Mo Green, 'foh The Man be bustin' our sorry asses."

Footsteps ran off.

Nathan groaned again.

Nausea and blackness.

Nathan blinked at two fuzzy faces. "Uh—"

His gasp was cut short by assorted hurting: the throbbing of his nose, a duller ache from the back of his head, and the much sharper pain of his side, like a sliver of steel lodged between the ribs under his right arm.

He threw up.

Even after catching his breath, Nathan couldn't speak. His throat and mouth burned from his own vile juices. All he could manage was a slight groan.

"Okay, okay, take it easy," one of the blurred faces said gruffly.

The other face leaned in closer, speaking in a soothing whisper, "You'll be okay, Nate, an ambulance is on its way. You aren't hurt too bad."

Not too bad? He felt like he'd been run over by a truck.

Nathan blinked, squinting through the veil of pain, trying to see clearly the woman behind the gentle voice. The fuzzy face slowly took shape: bright, dark eyes, big smile, and the whitest teeth. It was the young woman who worked over at St. Anthony's, who always spoke to him in her friendly, hoarse voice. He'd seen her that afternoon when he had eaten over there. Her nametag read...?

LuLu, that was it.

Nathan tried unsuccessfully to smile. Instead, he grimaced and groaned, his nose still dripping blood, his head still aching, and his right side, when he breathed deeply, feeling like someone was stabbing him with an ice pick.

The woman leaned closer, gently wiping his bloody face with a wet cloth of some kind. "Could've been a lot worse. That nutty Eug had a razor and would've cut your throat. This will help."

She lifted his head, putting something under to support it, and pushed the palm of her other hand squarely against his forehead.

Whoa!

Nathan flinched back from the unexpected sensation. It felt like he'd been hit with an icy lighting bolt right between the eyes the exact moment LuLu's bare palm had touched his skin. He groaned again, his vision tunneling as the electricity traveled from his head down his spine, cramping every muscle in his body. His back arched up violently—

Blackness.

Nathan awakened four hours later in the trauma center at San Francisco General Hospital, the nurses confirming LuLu's initial diagnosis that he wasn't hurt too badly and was in little danger from his assorted injuries, except for the possibility of a bad concussion. Black Angus and his buddies had broken Nathan's nose and cracked two ribs, but that was the extent of any serious damage. The back of his head and his chest were badly bruised, but internally he was only shaken up. Nathan made it through the night okay, until the announcement the next morning when the doctor came in with some preliminary test results. They'd done a CAT scan and an EEG as precautionary measures because of the concussion. Through a heavy drug haze, Nathan learned that he appeared to be okay physically, but his brain wave pattern was not quite normal. Instead, it resembled that of an epileptic. The doctor was not sure if this was caused by the recent beating or perhaps just his normal base. They wanted to keep him in the hospital, under medication, for a few days of more observation and testing.

The medical staff learned little from the additional tests, including a MRI, other than that the abnormal brain wave pattern was probably "normal" for Nathan. They would have preferred to study him more, but the city's main hospital for street people was understaffed and overworked, so the doctors reluctantly released him Wednesday afternoon with a prescription for Tylenol-codeine that Nathan never filled.

Oddly, from day one back on the street he experienced no withdrawal symptoms, no booze or dope calls. None. But on Wednesday night, back at Hotel Reo, Nathan experienced the first of his seizure-alterations after taking off his clothes for a warm sponge bath at the rust-stained sink in his room. The same thing recurred Thursday night. He wandered around, making faces and gestures at people who couldn't see him, laughing like a simple-minded fool.

The night after the jelly doughnut escapade, Nathan sat quietly on the foot of his bed, still trying to get a grip on the situation.

Obviously, he was a changed person, gifted with a special ability; a *better* person, if what had happened had permanently cured his drinking problem. Unfortunately, whatever was going on hadn't wiped out the previous decade. When he'd left the hospital after the accident ten years before, his wife and son gone, he'd taken up a new life in the Tenderloin and a new career as a stumblebum. A lifestyle not easy to shed.

Nathan shook his head, making up his mind to retain the memory of his wife and son, but realizing it was past time to let go of the guilt. That part of his life was over. Being a drunken bum did nothing for Geri or Davy except disgrace their memory. Maybe, with the special ability, he was being offered a second chance to turn his life around.

Nathan laughed at himself.

If he were being offered an escape from his sordid existence, he was indeed squandering it, wandering around making stupid faces at people who couldn't see him and stealing jelly doughnuts. He should be doing something more substantial, something that would allow him to rehabilitate himself, maybe escape the

Tenderloin, move on, do something significant with his remaining years.

The thought sobered Nathan.

What could he do with his special ability?

Like up at All-Star Donuts, he could walk into any place he liked and take whatever he needed. *Money!* The thought excited him.

Where?

Banks were his first thought.

But at night, when the transformation worked?

No. Besides, banks would cause an uproar and involve the media, the FBI.

What about groceries, liquor stores?

They'd raise a lot of attention too, and the cops...

The solution made him burst out with a laugh because it was so simple, and for sure there'd be no fuss afterward with the law.

He'd rob Dana 5-Diamond.

A Dealer Known as Dana 5-D

That afternoon, Nathan finally found the man he was looking for hanging out in front of the Korean grocery on the corner of Leavenworth and O'Farrell. Short Stuff. Double S.

"Hey, Nate, ya lookin' good, man, ya gettin' lotsa sun or somepin'," the legless black man on the scooterboard said, knuckling Nathan's fist. "Whassup?"

"Yeah, getting out and walking during the day and giving up the booze, man," Nathan explained, his tone serious. Double S had probably heard this a hundred times on the street, from a hundred dudes, with ninety-nine out of the hundred eventually backsliding. But Nathan meant what he said, and it probably showed in his eyes. The perceptive street hustler picked up on it.

Double S nodded, grinning broadly. "Agreein' wif ya, man. Right on!"

Nathan slipped the man a couple of bills. "Need some info, Double S. Where's Dana 5-Diamond's game tonight? And who's playing?"

The man squinted, eyeing Nathan curiously. "Ya don't plan on takin' up gamblin' now, do ya?"

Shaking his head, Nathan lied. "No. Location's for a friend of mine, gambler friend."

"Well he better be holdin', ya know what I'm sayin'?" Double S handed Nathan a note with the address scribbled down. "Buy-in ten large. Only one local, Herbie-the-Heist, an' three heavies comin' over the bridge from Oakland, unnerstan'?"

Nathan took the address and nodded. There would be lots of money in Dana 5-D's game, and fortunately he knew what the Herbie, the ex-bank robber, looked like. "Hey, thanks...for my friend," he said, with a sly smile.

Double S winked back.

Around 9:00 p.m. that night, Nathan waited beside a gated entry to an apartment building down on Taylor: eight stories high, recently painted, looking real nice. But still in the 'loin. Dana 5-D knew her roots.

After a few minutes, a black Chrysler limo pulled up and double-parked; the driver hustled out and around to open the back door. Herbie-the-Heist stepped out, hatless but wearing a classy grey herringbone topcoat. He stepped up to the gate, buzzed the bell, and growled something into the intercom.

The gate popped open. Unnoticed, Nathan closely followed the gambler into the building.

Inside a third floor apartment, Herbie paused just inside a large living room, taking off his coat as a jacketed big guy carefully swept him with a metal detector. Herbie was unarmed. Nathan slipped into the room behind him and looked around.

The dimly-lit place was sparsely furnished. A bar was set up against the wall next to a coat rack to the left of the door, manned by another jacketed husky man. Centered in the middle of the dark room stood a green-felted, hexagonal card table with drink wells. One shaded lamp hung down from the ceiling and shined brightly on the green felt, giving it the appearance of a pool table.

Dana 5-D was dealing, of course. Her huge bald-headed bodyguard, Pee Wee, stood right behind her. Stacks of red and blue chips were within easy reach to her right on the table, and on a chair beside the dealer's right knee was a closed dark grey tin box—the bank.

Herbie leaned across the table to hand the dealer his buy-in, a thin stack of banded hundreds. She stood to accept both them and his greeting.

"Dana, good to see you. You're looking gorgeous as usual."

The tall, pretty brunette's cheeks flushed. She sat back down, nodded and smiled, apparently embarrassed slightly by the off-hand compliment, but Nathan saw the green dollar signs momentarily register in her brown eyes, betraying the real source of her temporary loss of poise. Dana 5-D dropped the banded hundreds into the tin box and slid six stacks of chips across the table to an empty spot.

"Sit down there, Herb. You know everyone here?"

Herbie-the-Heist nodded and shook hands with the other three players from Oakland, who, like the ex-bank robber, were all middle-aged, nondescript white men wearing short sleeve dress shirts without ties. Their coats hung in a row by the bar; none of the men were familiar to Nathan.

"What are you drinking, Herb?" Dana 5-D asked, beckoning the bartender over.

"Bushmills and water," Herbie said, glancing around the table at the other men, their places marked by their stacks of chips and nearly-full glasses in the drink wells. He took the empty place indicated beside the dealer, making himself comfortable. Conspicuously missing from the table were ashtrays. No one was ever allowed to smoke at the table in a Dana 5-D game. Nathan grinned to himself, having counted on the well-known house rule in his simple game plan.

Unnoticed by anyone in the room, including Pee Wee and the other two obviously armed thugs, Nathan moved quietly around the table, stopping near the chair bearing the closed tin box, waiting for his moment.

At about ten-thirty, after a dozen or so hands, one of the Oakland players stood up, pulled a pack of Camels from his shirt pocket, and asked Dana 5-D, "Okay to take a smoke break?"

"In the hall outside," the dealer replied, standing up and stretching her distance-runner's body. "Restroom down the hall," she indicated to the other players.

As the gamblers all rose and shuffled around, Nathan snatched up the tin box, tucked it under his arm, and quietly followed the smoker to the door. The doorman unlocked it, leaned out and checked the hallway, then pointed out an urn down near the elevator. "Use that."

Nathan slipped out the door close behind the Oakland gambler, the tin box hugged tightly against his clear-taped ribs. In the hall, he walked quietly past the man lighting his cigarette near the elevator and continued a few steps to the stairwell. With his heart thumping, Nathan sprinted down the three flights of stairs, out the front door, and finally arrived onto Taylor Street before gasping for breath and looking back over his shoulder.

No one had followed.

On the street headed for home, Nathan couldn't restrain a loud laugh and a "Hooyaw!" that startled a pair of tall-legged transvestites loitering arm-in-arm near a white fire hydrant, waving at passing cars.

I really did it! Nathan thought, hurrying toward Jones Street and the safety of the Reo Hotel. It had been easy, a piece of cake.

A few steps from home Nathan slowed, suddenly aware of the creepy sensation of being watched…or followed. It raised the hair on the back of his neck. *Jesus, not now.*

He stopped suddenly and spun around.

There were plenty of people up and down Jones, but none of the three thugs from Dana 5-D's. No one else seemed to be paying any attention to him or the tin box he carried. Hell, how could they? No one could even see him, and the grey box was too dark to spot at a distance.

He ignored the lingering feeling and continued on to the hotel.

In his room, Nathan opened the box and quickly thumbed the banded money, spreading stacks of hundreds and fifties out on his bed. Fifty thousand dollars.

His elation over the successful robbery turned out to be short-lived. Sure, he had a lot of money, but he had no one to share it with, no friends, no family. He realized that his special ability isolated him, even more so than his ten years of drunkenness. He was one of a kind. A freak. The realization was depressing.

A scream from down the hall cut into his thoughts.

Still transformed, Nathan snatched up the small bat that he kept by his bed for protection, hurried down the darkened corridor, and pushed open the unlocked door to Sweet Jane's room.

A partially dressed man and the naked woman were struggling over a handful of money.

The small but stocky man punched the aging hooker solidly in the stomach, sending her flying backward onto her rumpled bed.

"I tole you, bitch, that your tired ass ain't worth no fifty bucks for all night," he said. His words slurred as he shook the fist of clenched money in the women's reddened face. "I'm leaving. Here, here's ten back." He tossed the bill on the bed at Sweet Jane's feet, scooping up his shirt from a chair but eyeing the weeping woman who curled up in a ball. "I oughtta really kick your lazy ass—"

Nathan slammed the child's bat against the back of the drunken john's head.

The man crumpled in a heap on the floor, unconscious.

Nathan peeled open the fist holding the money and tossed the bills next to the ten on the foot of the bed. Then he hooked his arms under the small man's arms, locking his hands on the man's chest, and dragged him out of the room, pausing momentarily to glance at Sweet Jane. She was still curled up crying quietly on her bed, unaware of what had happened. He closed the door before dragging the john down the hall to the stairwell.

After leaving the unconscious man in a heap in the lobby near the barred front desk—Ferdie would call the cops—Nathan returned to the third floor and his room for a minute. Then he tiptoed back down the hallway. He knelt quietly at Sweet Jane's door and listened. No crying sounds. He pushed the stacks of banded hundreds and fifties under the door with a note that read: *Time to leave the life; teach little girls to play the violin.*

Exhausted by the evening's excitement and exertions, Nathan returned to his room and managed to easily drop off to sleep.

That Creepy Feeling

The next evening, Nathan walked out of the Reo after dropping the curtain, pausing a moment and rubbing his arms and chest. The night was already foggy, the sidewalk and street damp. Sunday night; not much of a crowd out yet in the cool mist. Trying unsuccessfully to forget his nakedness, Nathan couldn't suppress a shiver. His bare footsteps made sticking sounds against the damp sidewalk as he absently wandered in the general direction of O'Farrell Street. He increased his speed, trying to warm up, then stopped suddenly, overwhelmed again by the feeling of being watched.

He glanced back.

An elderly Asian lady carrying a child hurried close behind him, but she didn't even glance his way as she passed by.

Nathan looked up, carefully scanning windows above the street level. There was no sign of the watcher. He knew it wasn't his imagination. Someone was watching him; someone nearby. *But who?*

Pee Wee? One of the other thugs?

He started walking slowly, his senses keenly alert.

Uh-huh, there.

He heard it, faintly but clearly: the sticking sound of footsteps following.

Nathan whirled around, expecting to surprise his stalker.

But the sidewalk was empty behind him for over half a block.

The faint sticking sounds continued approaching, drawing his gaze down to the wet sidewalk.

Footprints.

"Jesus," Nathan gasped aloud, watching as two distinct sets of foot imprints appeared on the damp sidewalk, walking directly toward him, only ten yards away. Both figures were completely invisible.

Heart thudding against his ribs, Nathan would have bolted if his legs hadn't suddenly betrayed him, turning to spaghetti. It was all he could do to remain standing. Still, after a deep breath, he managed to shuffle back a step, retreating from the advancing footprints.

"Wait," a voice whispered hoarsely as the footsteps closed in. "It's okay, Nate, we're your friends."

Despite being rattled, Nathan recognized the disembodied voice.

It was the St. Anthony's girl from the other night. LuLu.

Both sets of footprints stopped less than two feet away.

Just barely visible in the darkness, leaning up close, appeared two fuzzy dark faces.

"You're not alone," LuLu explained, "we are just like you—"

"W-what do you mean?" Nathan stammered, barely keeping his wits about him.

"Well, you're not one of a kind, Nathan," LuLu said. "There are three of us with the same special ability. You, Michael—the policeman, remember him?—and me."

"That's right," agreed a gruff male voice. "We are exactly like you."

"Uh-huh," Nathan said, his rapid pulse easing slightly. "*What* are we?" he asked bluntly. "Some kind of freaks?"

Both of the fuzzy shapes laughed and backed away, disappearing again from view.

"We are the next step in evolution, armed with a very special ability," LuLu said. "We've been waiting for you to exercise your latent skill, but you've been suppressing its emergence with your lifestyle, the drinking. But we've known for some time you were almost ready to join us. I helped at Homeboy's that night, giving you a jolt when I touched you while visualizing the curtain to myself. We've been following you closely ever since you left SF Gen, waiting for you to answer a question we had about your nerve. You answered it last night. Man, you definitely have guts, ripping off Dana 5-D and her stooges right under their noses, without even a weapon."

"How did you recognize me as one of you?" Nathan said, still shaken by what he was hearing. Before either answered, he added, "How could you follow me if I can't be seen?"

"We may not be able to see each other except up very close, but we can *recognize* each other's presence," the gruff voice replied. "Close your eyes, face our direction, and relax."

Nathan followed Michael's instructions. After squeezing his eyes shut, he felt an odd sensation, a kind of warmth generating the distinct images of two individual figures in his mind—a sixth sense? He blinked.

Michael said, "You see, no one else can sense our presence when the curtain is dropped, only one of us three, and only at very close range—no more than fifteen yards."

"I know how you must feel, Nathan, a little overwhelmed by the uniqueness of all this," LuLu said.

"The curtain, what about it?" Nathan asked, beginning to calm down as their answers made sense of what had been happening to him the past four days.

LuLu chuckled again. "Well, it's just a mental triggering device to activate the physical skin change and transformed state," she said, her voice growing serious. "A state Michael and I can maintain for about ninety minutes after months of practice. But you, Nate, already you are able to drop the curtain for four or more hours. With this much ability, you can't be wasting time robbing gamblers. No, the city is full of many more dangerous predators, preying on the weak and poor. *Garbage.* We hope you will lead us in a big clean-up, beginning here in the Tenderloin— an undercover, low-key operation."

"Yeah, man," Michael added gruffly. "We start tonight."

Nathan noticed something shiny hovering in the nearby shadows, three black-enameled nightsticks. Michael smacked them loudly into his invisible hand and said, "We are going to start with three scumbag crack dealers up at Homeboy's. Remember them? Uh-huh, skull thumping time. Here."

As he clasped the weapon in hand, Nathan felt a surge of power race through his veins, as if the baton were really the magic sword Excalibur. The sense of empowerment was accompanied by a strong feeling, almost like a booze call, a craving; but for what?

Revenge, he thought, grinning wryly to himself. He closely followed his companions' wet footsteps up the street. No, it was more than simple payback for the beating he'd received, more than petty vindication for all the indignities suffered for ten years. LuLu was right: it was time to begin a vigilante cleanup, time to permanently remove the garbage from the Tenderloin.

"Yes, indeed," Nathan McKee said aloud with fierce enthusiasm. His footsteps took the lead, guiding his invisible cohorts toward Homeboy's and the beginning of The Cleansing.

BRUISED SOUL

You have only one friend in the ring, boyo: a clinch!
—Danny Boy Doyle

Micky D saw a Visitor his first night back in the Tenderloin, but at the time he didn't recognize her as one of them.

He'd finally made it to the address on Jones Street just off O'Farrell around ten o'clock at night on Monday—the time of heavy buying and selling in the 'loin. He paused halfway up the steps of the six-story building, turned and listened to the din of traffic for a moment, then looked back down on some of the street people roaming Jones like stray dogs: skimpily-dressed hookers, furtive dealers, dead-eyed junkies, shuffling winos, fast-talking hustlers, and the smelly homeless. The forgotten and the never known. *The faces change*, he thought, smiling wryly, *but no one ever escapes.* But what about him? He shrugged his shoulders, sucked in a deep breath, and lingered for another moment, letting the early summer fog creeping in from San Francisco Bay whirl around him, hoping the familiar sights and sounds and smells and mist would help dampen the jittery edge he'd developed on the long Greyhound bus ride. He felt wound pretty tight, like in the early days of anxiously waiting for his trainer, Danny Boy, to tape his hands before a four-rounder. His vision was tunneling slightly, but he hadn't seen or heard anything really weird. Still, he could almost hear Dr. Gee's warning: *Michael, remember to take your meds religiously at breakfast, lunch, and dinner.*

Of course it was long past the five o'clock dinner hour up at Napa State Hospital, and he hadn't eaten since breakfast. Even though he'd been released from the hospital before noon, there'd been no Greyhound service out of Napa. He'd waited and bummed a ride with one of the psych techs from his ward who got off at four o'clock and lived in Vallejo. He'd caught a bus out of there at six-thirty, making long stops in Richmond and Berkeley before finally heading west on the last leg across the Bay Bridge and into the city.

He turned and climbed the remaining front steps, and then rang the manager's bell—apartment two, main floor. Cecil Robinson had been eating, but he answered the door quickly. He wiped his mouth, introduced himself, and gave Micky D his key along with all the "dos and don'ts" before directing him up the stairwell.

"'Member, mon, no smokin' inna buildin'," the manager repeated in his lilting Caribbean English. "Go up on de roof if ya gonna blow one, ya hear me?"

He nodded and slipped past the heavyset black man, through the strong smell of curry that clung to the walls of the dingy hallway.

"That's all ya stuff?"

Micky D looked back over his shoulder and said, "Yeah, that's it." He held up his old training bag, no larger than the normal airline carry-on. He hadn't accumulated much in his six-month stay at the state hospital.

He climbed the narrow staircase to the sixth floor, checking the apartment numbers on the doors to the left as he walked down the hallway. His place, number sixty-six, must be the last one near the roof stairs.

Just after he had inserted his key and fiddled with the sticky lock, a woman came along the hall leading a young man. She paused in front of the door across from Micky D, number sixty-five, and smiled. "You must be my new neighbor," she said, her voice strangely accented and smoky.

He nodded.

The woman held out her hand. It was cold to the touch. "Nice to meet you," she said warmly, handing her key to the young man behind her. "Go on in, sweetie," she instructed the guy, who glanced away shyly as he slid by, unlocked the door, and disappeared into her apartment.

"I'm Jen-na," she said to Micky D, dividing the name into distinct syllables.

He nodded back. "They call me Micky D," he said, letting her hand slip from his fingers.

She was tall, at least six feet, heavily bundled in a greyish overcoat and thick black scarf. Her buzz-clipped hair was almost white, her face pale and gaunt but not unattractive, and her eyes were her most distinctive feature—almond shaped, almost Asian, but with nearly colorless irises. Just a trace of blue, like clouded ice. Even though the woman was smiling in a friendly manner, Micky D couldn't help but feel slightly unsettled because her unwavering gaze was aggressive and penetrating, almost predatory. Usually people were less assertive when first meeting him. They found his rugged, prize-fighter features with the prominent scar tissue over both eyes and his badly broken nose scary. He knew it was a face that didn't encourage argument.

As if privy to the unnerving impact her own unusual appearance and gaze aroused, she chuckled and said, "Nice to meet you Micky D," then spun gracefully on her heel, glided to her door, and added, "but now I have a guest to, ah, instruct." She followed the young man into her apartment, leaving Micky D staring at the number sixty-five on her door.

Wonder what exactly she teaches? he asked himself, finding the woman's exotic features, elegant movement, and gravelly voice very attractive. Her peculiar accent added to the intrigue because he couldn't quite place it. Surely not Asian...perhaps Eastern European. One thing he was certain of: even though he'd never met her before, there was something vaguely familiar about Jenna. His nerves were strung too tight after the wearing trip and unsettling encounter; he wasn't thinking clearly. It would come to him.

He unlocked his door and checked out the small furnished studio. A bed, a closet, a dresser, and a tiny toilet with shower and sink were all it contained. Spartan, but surprisingly clean.

He fumbled through his duffel and found his pill bottles. Cupping a drink of water in his hand, he washed down two meds: lithium and the substitution for chlorpromazine—olanzapine. Dr. Gee had thought the new combination would have fewer energy-sapping side effects. So far the psychiatrist was wrong. The psychotropic drugs made him sluggish both mentally and physically. After another gulp of water, Micky D went to the only window and looked down on busy Jones Street. He was pretty familiar with this location; six months ago he'd lived around the corner and down two blocks on O'Farrell in a residential hotel.

Yeah, there was the laundromat up the block on Jones where he'd been picked up by the cops, staring fixedly for almost four hours at his laundry tumbling over and over in a dryer, moving only to stick a steady stream of quarters in the machine, coins he'd apparently scooped up from the bill changer he'd battered. A concerned Vietnamese lady had finally called 911. He vaguely remembered the cops bringing his caseworker from social services, Ms. Fingerson. Then time had gotten fucked up, flashing by in a blur, like his life had been continuously on fast-forward. He had come around briefly several weeks later up in Napa, locked down in a secured ward at the hospital with mostly PCPs—penal code patients—from San Quentin and Atascadero.

He took another deep breath. At the moment he needed to wash off the clammy grime, get a grip on himself, and catch some needed rest. Tomorrow he'd find out about Jane, then he might check out the Harrison Street Gym and look up his old manager. He probably should go over to the Mission and meet his new caseworker, Mr. Rollo. He needed to see about food vouchers, because he only had about ten bucks in cash.

Oh yeah, the meds were kicking in on his empty stomach, making him feel fuzzy-headed and drifty.

With the numbing effect of his pills, Micky D dropped off to sleep fairly quickly, but only after listening for a few minutes to whispering, giggling, moaning, and groaning sounds coming from across the hall. Then there was the drawn-out, throaty, "Oh yeah..." when he got up to go to the bathroom at three or so. Sexually stimulating sounds. Something Micky D hadn't felt in some time.

When he finally roused himself from deep sleep, it was mid-morning. He decided he'd first go out and run down his partner, Blue, before heading over to Harrison Street. As he was leaving his apartment the door opened to number sixty-five, and the appearance of the man that exited surprised Micky D. It wasn't the shy young dude from the previous night; instead, an old man, slumped-shouldered and grey-headed, shuffled off down the hall. What the hell was he doing at Jenna's? Certainly not making any of those panting and moaning sounds. Maybe she *was* really teaching something to an early morning student, Micky D decided as the old guy disappeared down the stairwell. For just a moment he debated knocking on the young woman's door, checking out how she looked this morning after all her noisy instruction. But he couldn't come up with a good excuse, so he just smiled dryly as he trucked on out to the street, thinking he might need some of whatever she was teaching for himself.

It was a great San Francisco morning, bright and clear, quiet with most everyone still inside and off the street. The lingering smell of bacon frying somewhere nearby made his stomach growl. He hoofed it down to Homeboy's near the corner of Leavenworth and O'Farrell, but it was boarded up, apparently out of business since Micky D had been away. He thought for a minute, then turned and climbed the hill back up near Van Ness to the Korean's, where he finally spotted Blue, hanging out in front of the liquor store.

The thinly-built Army Ranger veteran, a long-time fight fan, had been Micky D's closest friend for over two years, ever since Blue had come to the 'loin after getting out of the VA hospital over in Martinez. He'd lost part of his lower right leg to a mine in Afghanistan, but after being released from the hospital, he'd received a pretty good disability pension and some other benefits like counseling and prescription drugs from the VA clinic near the Presidio.

"Hey, man," Micky D said, walking up to his tall, black friend, who still wore the same skimpy goatee and old Army fatigue jacket with the Ranger patch he'd worn when Micky D had last seen him. "What's happening?"

Blue, grinning broadly, tapped Micky D's closed fist, shook his hand, and hugged him tightly. "Yo, dude, when did the 'rales raise you?"

"Got in on the bus late last night," Micky D answered, checking his buddy out. Blue was still too skinny, but his eyes were clear, his gaze steady, and he looked healthy. He looked like he was doing okay. "I appreciate you dropping the bread in my canteen account at the hospital. It helped, man, but why didn't you ever send me a card or letter?"

Blue rubbed his nose, looking a little sheepish, and said, "Oh, you know me, dude. Actually, a couple times I considered rounding up the boys and cutting a disc at Trey's, but I wasn't sure they would even let you hear it up there."

"Well, thanks anyhow," Micky D said, sighing and pushing his hands deep in his pockets as he looked down at his feet. He'd put off the question he dreaded long enough. "Say, Blue, you seen Sweet Jane around? Both my letters addressed to our old place down on O'Farrell bounced back marked 'Moved Left No Forward.'"

Blue's grin quickly changed to a hurting frown, like someone had suddenly whacked his stump just above his prosthetic lower right leg.

"Ah, man, guess you ain't heard. Things got real bad with Janey soon after you left. She really got strung out. Kept talking about getting back on methadone, you know. Instead, she lost her dancing gig and your place, ended up over on Capp Street, maybe three months ago."

At that, Micky D stiffened slightly. Capp Street was the absolute end of the line for someone like Jane with a serious habit and out of work. Cheap hooker city.

Blue cleared his throat, his expression still pained. "But there's more bad news, man," he continued in a husky tone, "and I hate to be the one to drop this on you, pal, but Janey OD'd 'bout eight weeks ago." Blue looked down at his feet, smiling thinly. "Few of us had a little memorial after the city put her down, you know. We went over to Trey's, slammed down a few of them Polish vodkas she liked when she was flush. Everybody did a little rap about her biting wit, or great wheels, or cool dancing and all—kinda nice, you know, considering," Blue paused, then looked his friend in the eye and held his hands palms up with an apologetic shrug, as if to say, *What else could we do?*

"I know, I know," Micky D mumbled. He nodded, trying to examine his feelings like he'd been taught in group at Napa.

He wasn't really surprised about Jane. He'd suspected something like that had probably gone down. To be honest, he didn't really feel all that torn up, just sort of numbed except for a twinge of guilt for not being there. She hadn't written after his first month, and when his letters had started coming back, he'd assumed she'd gone out again. They'd lived together on O'Farrell, and at first he'd done pretty well, keeping her away from the junk, on methadone maintenance. Until the end, there. Jane, with all her problems, had probably kept him on the street six months or so longer than he'd deserved, paying most of their bills from her exotic dancing gigs up at the Mitchell Brothers after the last of his boxing money ran out. But she'd been unable to permanently prolong his slide. A month or so before that last day, he'd been having funny spells, wandering around in a daze, getting paranoid, getting involved in several dust-ups with the law. But it had been an awkward relationship with Jane from the beginning, constant fighting over everything, both of them stubbornly clinging to their dreams: Micky D getting back his boxing license, Jane hooking up with a musical in the legit theater. Up and down for three years, a relationship of habit and convenience more than love, knowing it would probably end badly for one of them. He'd expected it to be him. Jane had been so tough, a survivor. But now he realized it had been slipping away from her, too, as he'd gradually sunk down into his own black despair.

He stared off idly down O'Farrell, watching a derelict hold a conversation with a parking meter, still thinking about the doomed relationship with Jane. He'd actually been doing both their laundry at the Jones Street Laundromat when he'd slipped into the abyss. Funny, as screwed up as he'd been that day, he could still remember every item of her stuff flopping around in that dryer: five pairs of panties, one blue, one black, three white; two University of San Francisco faded green T-shirts; a white bra; three pairs of socks; and her raggedy-ass grey sweat pants and shirt.

"Sorry, man," Blue said in a respectful whisper.

It was quiet for a few minutes after that as Blue gave Micky D some space and time to process the bad news.

A guy wearing the greasy, multi-layered attire of the homeless limped up, opening and extending his dirty hand, which was full of small change—mostly pennies. "Can ya guys help me out this mornin'?" he asked in a defeated tone. "I need another ten cents to catch the bus over to the free clinic."

Blue pulled a quarter out of his pocket and dropped it into the guy's hand, shooing him away.

"Thanks, man," the bum said, grinning and clutching his fist full of happiness tightly. Then he hurried into the Korean's to pick up his morning taste.

Finally, Micky D blew his nose, sucked in a deep breath, and suggested in a hoarse voice, "So, Blue, maybe we should go over to St. Anthony's. I haven't eaten since sometime early yesterday, and I'm starving but almost broke."

"Hey, let me get you a sandwich here at the Korean's," Blue volunteered.

At the end of the month, when they were low on cash, the two friends had worked out a good hustle. Blue would dig out his old, battered silver sax, then they'd truck on down to Pier 39 in the afternoon when the wharf was thick with tourists. Blue would take off his prosthetic leg, sit, and play some funky blues or jazz and Micky D would pass the hat. The soulful music by a disabled vet and Micky D's no-nonsense face encouraged the tourists to dig deep. Usually in an hour—sometimes less—they would have a hundred bucks in the hat, enough to get them by until the first of the month. But it was a gig they could only manage to organize when seriously pressed for cash.

It didn't take long this time before the hat had enough to get what they needed and they were sitting on some cardboard in the nearby alley with a couple of ham and egg sandwiches and a bottle of wine. Blue liked to drink white port, squirting in a taste of lemon juice from one of those yellow plastic bulbs. When he first passed the bottle and a Styrofoam cup, Micky D hesitated, hearing Dr. Gee's stern admonition: *No booze, Michael. And absolutely no street drugs.*

But after what he'd confirmed about Sweet Jane, and especially his shameful lack of real feeling about it, he cut off the medical advice and took the bottle, trying to drown the lingering trace of his guilt.

They ate the sandwiches, caught up on old times, and drank wine for the rest of the morning.

After they scored a hundred and forty-seven bucks with their sax gig on Tuesday afternoon, Micky D sank into a pattern as the next few days rolled by: sleep late, find Blue, then hang out and drink more and more. He put off plans to see his new caseworker until Friday. Taking his meds only at night helped keep his thinking clear during the day and restored a little attitude to his walk. After talking it over with Blue, he had every intention of going over to the Harrison Street Gym and getting back in shape...real soon. He was only thirty-four, and with proper medical clearance there was a good chance he could get his license back from the state. Who knew, maybe he had another championship fight still in him.

Friday, Micky D made it over to see Mr. Rollo at Social Services. He filled out the forms to get temporary assistance until his SSI kicked back in, picked up some rent and food vouchers, and came back to the 'loin feeling pretty good. He still hadn't checked into psychiatric outpatient services at UCSF Hospital as he'd promised Dr. Gee, but that could wait. Shoot, his head was even clearer than before the MRI had revealed the cerebral bleeding after the championship bout three years before. No weird thoughts at all, and he sure as hell wasn't hearing or seeing anything strange...at least nothing stranger than the normal weird shit in the 'loin.

His key stuck, and he rattled his door impatiently. Across from him, Jenna cracked her door and peeked out into the hallway, all bundled up in her coat and scarf.

"Ah, Mr. Micky D," she said, extending her hand. "My current guest just disappeared out the door a moment ago. Their coming and going at all hours bothering you?"

When he took her hand, he felt an electrical jolt; his whole arm tingled. It reminded Micky D of a ninth-grade science experiment when they all held hands in a circle while the teacher cranked up a magneto hooked up to them. Back then, a tingling electrical charge had run up one arm, across his shoulders, and down his other arm to the next person. This was the same jazzy feeling, only kind of sexy, too. Jenna smiled as if she knew, the nostrils of her finely shaped nose sort of pinched like she was peeking outside into weather below zero. Her lips were full, sensuous. And her beautiful eyes...Jesus, it'd been a long time.

"Micky D, you didn't answer."

"Oh," he said, blinking and stammering. "I-I...no, your guests aren't bothering me." But the late night moaning...

Unobserved by Micky D, someone had walked up on them from the direction of the roof stairwell: a young guy wearing a black and silver Raiders jacket, a thick mop of unruly red hair, and an expression full of confident attitude. "Hi," he said to Micky D, grabbing one of Jenna's hands. "Fog's coming in, babe, it's getting too cool for the roof," he announced to her.

She nodded and shivered. "Let's go back in, do something to warm up." She backed up and cracked the door wider. A humid gush of tropical air escaped and hit Micky D in the face almost as hard as a left jab. "Bye," she said as she disappeared with her red-headed guest.

Micky D stood for several minutes until he heard the first of the intimate sounds beginning. It was Jenna making most of the noise. He couldn't help wondering what she looked like without the coat and scarf.

The next morning he left his apartment just as the door to sixty-five opened to let out the guy wearing the silver and black jacket. His appearance shocked Micky D. The unruly red hair was heavily streaked with grey, and the young man had aged at least forty years. His confident expression was gone, and he avoided eye contact with Micky D as he limped off down the hall.

"Jesus," Micky D swore under his breath. He snapped his fingers and stared at Jenna's apartment door, realizing why she had struck him as so familiar. Sure, there was a familiarity to her face, her pinched nostrils, and the clouded-ice eyes, but the sight of the transformed guy triggered the recall. Just like Rashad had described up in P Ward at the hospital.

Jenna was one of the Visitors.

They'd been playing dominoes in the rec room, but had stopped to listen to Rashad when he had begun to talk about meeting an alien.

"Well, maybe not exactly an alien," Rashad said, struggling to control his high-pitched excitement. He looked across the table at Micky D. "She told my next door neighbor, Petey, that she actually came from the future, a time of a big red sun, where it was really muggy hot and everybody lived underground. A bunch of them were here in the Bay Area, collecting energy. She called them Visitors. Like I said, she was scary-looking, man. Platinum hair, piercing icy eyes, pinched nostrils, pale, bundled up and always cold, you know. And what she did to my friend and all them other guys…" Rashad's voice trailed off.

"What did she do?" Micky D asked, putting the dominoes away. The game was over for the day; after his rap, Rashad would be too jumpy to concentrate and play.

"Well, she was sucking the life out of them—"

"You mean like a vampire?"

"Nah, not exactly, not blood, but their youth, you know; like these young guys would go into her apartment and come out old men."

Micky D just kept quiet.

"She was screwing them silly, but somehow sucking all the youth out of them in the process." Rashad's brow was wrinkled deeply; his eyes looked off into space, obviously vividly picturing the memory. "Yeah, and she finally got poor Petey, too. Jumped his bones and put thirty years on him. But it must've been worth it, because after I saw him that last night when he looked to be fifty-five or sixty, he said he was going home with her."

"Home?"

"Yeah, the future, or another dimension, or wherever the fuck she came from, you know."

After that, Rashad kind of sagged at the table as if just the memory of the Visitor had sucked the life out of him.

"Well, what actually happened to your friend?"

"There was a fire in her apartment that last night," Rashad said, looking off again at the green ward wall. "I got to her place quickly, but it was empty." He shrugged. "That was it, man."

"What do you mean, that was it?" Micky D said, irritated by the abrupt conclusion of the story.

"They never found either of their bodies," Rashad said, sighing. "She'd obviously taken him home. The life force she'd claimed from Petey and them other guys, maybe even the fire, helped provide the energy she needed to transport them both. I'm not exactly sure of the mechanics. But I am sure that she was one of them Visitors."

At the time Micky D had just dismissed the story as no more crazy than others he'd heard or would hear at Napa in his six months there. But now, staring at the door to apartment sixty-five, he knew Rashad's story was true. Jenna was indeed one of the Visitors.

Jesus, he had to tell someone right away.

But who?

The cops? His caseworker?

He'd be back up to Napa in a New York minute if he went to them with a story about Jenna being a Visitor from the future.

Blue. He had to tell Blue.

But as Micky D left his building, he heard multiple sirens up near Van Ness, wailing like wounded animals.

He hurried up the climb on O'Farrell and saw a group clustered at the mouth of the alley just down from the Korean's. Cops. And an ambulance easing through the crowd of gawkers. Micky D followed, finally spotting someone doubled up with his face to the ground. Micky D could make out the Ranger patch on the guy's green Army jacket, and the sight made him suck in a deep breath. *No, it can't be,* he thought.

He pressed closer.

A cop rolled the guy over.

It *was* Blue.

"Let me in," he cried, trying to push closer. He saw the chest of his friend's jacket soaked with blood. "That's my buddy."

"Whoa," a cop said, roughly pushing Micky D back. "Give us room here, pal. This is a crime scene."

"Yo, Micky D," someone said, tugging at his pant leg.

It was Short Stuff, a legless guy sitting on his scooterboard, shaking his head sadly at Micky D. "Too late, dawg. Blue gone."

Stunned, Micky D shifted to keep his friend in view as the EMTs checked Blue. He managed a hoarse whisper. "What happened, Double S?"

The legless man shook his head sadly and said, "C'mon back here, man, where we kin hear. I'll tell ya."

Micky D followed Short Stuff back beyond the edge of the crowd. Double S stopped and passed up a small brown paper bag from his lap. "Take a heavy hit, man."

Micky D gulped down a fiery drink from the half-pint of Wild Irish Rose. The cheap whisky burned all the way to his gut. Another hit and the warmth began to spread out from his belly. He nodded gratefully.

Double S took the bag back, fortified himself, then began to explain what had happened. "Blue been runnin' a little bidness onna side, las' six months or so since ya'll been down. Scorin' extra scripshun meds from other vets at the clinic—vikes, oxies, whatever. Street dealin' here at the Korean's, ya unnerstan' what I'm tellin' ya?"

"I'm with you," Micky D said, his throat still raw from the whisky.

"Well, dude hit on him this mornin' an' Blue ain't holdin', ya see. Dude goes off, gets up in Blue's face. Blue pushes him, dude whips out a blade." Double S paused to lubricate his vocal cords with some more of the Rose. "Blue's number up, man, 'cuz the dude stuck him right in the heart. Dead 'foh the Man got here, ya know what I'm sayin'?"

"Ah, Jesus," Micky D murmured under his breath as he watched them load the covered body into the ambulance.

"Keep it fo' the las' taste, Micky D," Double S said, handing him the brown bag.

Micky D tapped the legless man's fist as he turned and walked away from the noisy scene, his vision tunneling down. But his feelings deep inside? Not much more than the brief twinge of guilt he'd felt hearing about Sweet Jane. His eyes were dry.

Man, something must be wrong with me, he thought. Maybe the Puerto Rican had bruised more than his brain the night of the championship, scarred something deep inside him, hurt his ability to feel much of anything. Or maybe it had happened gradually, over the course of his professional career—an accumulation of damage. A lot of veteran fighters worried about that, constantly reminded of the possibility by the slurred, drunken speech of the old punchies hanging around the gyms. But this wasn't the Parkinson's syndrome thing, he decided; it was more like he'd finally lost the capacity to really care. If so, he knew Dr. Gee wasn't going to be able to fix it with any therapy or pills. No way, man. What could anyone do for a seriously battered and scarred soul?

Even without taking his meds, Micky D slept all day and late into the night.

Thumping.

Loud knocking.

Someone shouting.

The sounds distorted, like distant echoes in a long tunnel.

Micky D struggled up into consciousness like a drowning man breaking the surface in murky water. He finally burst into the waking world, gasping greedily. His body was covered in clammy sweat, his heart pounding, his stomach muscles clenched in a painful knot.

"Mista Donahue, Mista Donahue!" Someone was shouting and hammering away at his apartment door.

Micky D escaped from the tangled damp sheets and trudged across the darkened room in his shorts. He pulled open the door and faced the heavyset manager, Mr. Robinson. His shiny face was agitated as he stood in the hall, fog swirling about him. "Come quick, mon!" he said, too loudly.

"What—?"

It wasn't fog out there, it was smoke. Choking clouds of it engulfed the hallway. How could he have slept through a fire?

The manager pointed down the hall to the stairs, sputtering almost incoherently, "Grab ya pants, get out."

"Okay," Micky D said. He found his jeans and shower shoes and slipped them on, then he made it back to the door.

"I gotta leave now," the manager explained, "help de old ones down lower."

Micky D nodded his understanding, then pointed across the hall at the closed door to apartment sixty-five. "What about Jenna?"

The manager, looking confused, shook his head. "Nobody live over dere."

"Yes, there is!"

Stepping across the hallway, Micky D ripped open the unlocked door to sixty-five and stepped into the smoke-filled apartment.

No one, nothing there except bare floors and fire crackling everywhere.

The manager coughed and covered his mouth with a handkerchief, mumbling, "Now we gotta go. Sixty-five vacant, no one livin' dere in a week." He grabbed Micky D's arm.

But Micky D pulled free, squinting in the smoke. "There was a woman here yesterday," he insisted.

The manager shook his head, his eyes widening as he reached out again for Micky D's arm. "Please, Mista Donahue. Mus' go now. No one dere!"

Jesus, could he have imagined the whole fucking thing? Micky D held his ground, staring into the vacant apartment. Jenna, her guests, the wild sex sounds? Even Rashad's explanation?

No.

Pulse racing, he turned away from the frightened fat man, squinting and glancing first down the smoke-filled hallway, then back toward the roof stairwell.

That's when he saw it, lying there in the hall near the roof stairs: the heavy black scarf.

"She's still here!" he said, stumbling away from the confused Mr. Robinson.

He ran up the stairs and out onto the roof, looking about frantically. The top of the building was completely engulfed in thick, dark smoke and scattered clusters of fire. He couldn't see ten feet in any direction. The intense heat from nearby flames made him flinch back. Glancing around anxiously, he figured he had sixty seconds at most to find Jenna and get her to the main stairwell or they'd be trapped. Desperate, he shouted out into the raging holocaust, "Jenna, Jenna, where are you?"

From somewhere across from him in the smoke, he heard her answer over the roaring sound of the fire. "Micky D! Over here!"

He dashed breathlessly across the roof to the Jones Street side, juking like an NFL running back, avoiding burning obstacles and a sudden column of fire that shot out of a broken skylight like a flamethrower. He finally spotted her—

Jesus.

She stood casually in the flames that leapt up off the side of the roof, smiling.

It was Jenna, shed of her overcoat, wearing a funny round backpack and dressed in some type of one-piece, skin-tight, high-necked metallic garment that glowed with a cool blue luminescence. It hid none of her finely shaped body. She beckoned to him, defying gravity like a large bird hovering on an upsweep of hot air.

Warily, he moved closer to the fiery edge of the building.

She leaned toward him, extending both hands, her eyes glittering with excitement. "Come with me, Micky D. Time to go home."

Home?

Whoa.

He drew back away from the woman's grasp, his vision tunneling down to a pinpoint as questions spun in his head like the smoke around him swirled in the wind.

Where?

Another dimension?

An alien world?

The distant future?

And going with an alien? A Visitor?

Below them, six stories down on Jones Street, a fire engine braked, its siren slowly winding down. Off in the distance, back-up engines shrieked loudly, answering its dying cry.

Gazing into Jenna's steady and beautiful eyes, Micky D inched closer, his pulse racing wildly.

Why not go? he asked himself. *What difference does it make?*

He cared about nothing and no one anymore.

Nothing.

He reached out and grasped her warm, warm hands.

Finally, Micky D sucked in a deep breath, steeled himself, and stepped out and away from the building's ledge…to join the gorgeous Visitor.

5150

W e got the call Friday night at 11:45 p.m.

"Car 3256, we have several reports of a black male acting oddly, highly agitated, scaring people…repeat, a code 5150 on Leavenworth between Post and Geary."

A 5150: a psycho, someone behaving in a threatening and irrational manner, or a situation gone completely ballistic, everything dangerously awry—a call every cop dreads more than testing positive for an STD.

"God Al-migh-ty," I panted under my breath, closing my eyes. The iceworm awakened in my gut and started feeding in an enraged frenzy, each electric crunch sending a bolt of icy pain tearing through my body. *The iceworm,* my special name for the ferocious little demon burrowed deeply in my lower intestine.

I gasped loudly.

Somehow, ingrained habits kicked in automatically. I sucked in a long, deep breath, squeezed my eyes even tighter, concentrated on a bright white dot for several seconds, then let the air trickle back out of my mouth and regained some degree of control. Blinking away the tears of pain, I reluctantly responded back to central dispatch in a shaky, hoarse voice: "Yeah, 10…4, this is car 3256 responding to the 5150, over and out."

My partner, Benny Tomaho, stomped the brakes on our patrol car, spun a fishtailing U on busy Geary Street, and headed back toward Leavenworth, hitting both the siren and flash bar and narrowly missing a long-legged tranny hooker stepping off the median. She gave us the finger as we sped by.

With a trembling hand I reached under the car seat, pulled out the Crystal Geyser liter bottle, and took a long pull. The high-proof cheap vodka made my eyes water, and it wasn't the first or second drink of the shift, even counting by fours. The huge hit of fiery liquor burned all the way down, the anesthetizing wave working itself out from my gut into my legs, arms, fingertips, and toes. For a moment or two I thought even my nose numbed. But I knew from past experience that the relaxed feeling from the jolt of vodka wouldn't last long, not permanently stilling the famished devil. No, the iceworm was locked in deep inside me, and no amount of booze or anything else would ever kill or dislodge it. At best, I could hope for only temporary respite, pray that it would be knocked out and stay asleep for awhile.

"Motherfuck," Benny said, oblivious to my pain, as he worked his way through the Tenderloin traffic. We were still a couple of blocks away from the location. "Only fifteen friggin' minutes until end of shift, Skipper. Then we would've busted out for two days, free from this miserable, sleazy, smelly armpit of the city."

Forget that weekend respite shit; small potatoes. I was close to permanent relief, 24/7. Two weeks—ten working days—until retirement from the San Francisco Police Department. Man, I was shorter than a mosquito's pecker. So *please*, I pleaded silently to a higher power, not some crazy-ass crap, not now, just a few nights before my escape from this ongoing nightmare.

"Wow, look at the size of that mob," Benny said, his higher-pitched-than-normal voice interrupting my self-pity. He braked a half block up Leavenworth from Geary, near Post Street, in front of the crowded alley entry. "Yeah, somebody has got to be down. C'mon, Skip!"

Benny jumped out of the car, pausing a few seconds to attach his baton and adjust his equipment belt.

I hung back long enough to scrunch down partially out of view of the crowd and take another swallow from the water bottle. I wiped my eyes and coughed. The little hit didn't help much with the fucking worm fully awake and chomping away sharply.

With an effort of will I forced myself out of the car, my weak knees almost buckling under me. For a moment I steadied myself against the side of the patrol car. Then, letting Benny take the lead, I followed, shouldering slowly through the crowd clustered at the mouth of the dark alley, noticing thankfully the lack of any immediate gunfire. Still, I moved stiffly, scanning left and right, *5150* repeating silently in my head. In short, "showing a lotta white eyeball," as the guys back at the station said, describing a rookie on an edgy call.

"Yo, Skip."

I glanced down to where I had almost stepped on the legless black guy resting on his scooterboard. He tugged at my pants leg.

"Hey, Double S," I said sheepishly, reaching down and tapping my knuckles against Short Stuff's fist, relieved to see someone in the crowd I knew well. "What's up? We got a 5150 a minute ago from dispatch."

Double S was a hustler, knew everything that happened on the street in the 'loin; you could bet a bundle he'd know what had gone down.

"Yeah, it be The Prophet got hisself hit, Skip," Short Stuff explained in a low whisper as I watched my partner continue working his way through the gawkers. He finally dropped alongside a man stretched out on his back in the alley. "He hasslin' wunna Big Leroy's ladies, Li'l Sister, and her john. You know his line, calling the dude somepin terrible, a...a forn-i-cator this time. Then on with his usual pocket-leaps rant, swearin' that shitstorm be hittin' the 'loin real soon. The dead be raisin' up, rippin'-n-runnin' like a mob of dope-sick junkie muthahfuckahs lookin' fo' a quick fix. Ya unnerstan' what I'm tellin' ya here, Skip? The dude was goin' off big time, barkin' and spittin' and pokin' his finger in this here john's face."

"Yeah, I hear you, Double S," I replied, nervously checking the crowd. I kept my eyes open for anyone looking hostile or coming my way with his hands jammed in his pockets.

"But The Prophet ain't lettin' it go, man, shakin' it like a pit bull wif a mailman's trouser leg in his mouf," Short Stuff said. "He callin' that john a whoremonger and Li'l Sister a jezebel, bof big time sinners in this here modern-day Sodomy and Gonorrhea, which was gonna bring on that pocket-leaps shit any day now."

Double S paused to take a breath and spit in the gutter. He looked around furtively before continuing. "Dick-shriveled the trick big time, ya know what I'm sayin'? John jus' turned away from Li'l Sister and hauled ass outta there, like my man Carl Lewis. And Big Leroy jus' up the street glarin', hearin' ever word of that rantin' and ravin' bullshit by The Prophet, jus' as plain as bad bref on a wino behind a Sterno binge."

"Pissed off Big Leroy," I said, peering over the heads of the crowd, searching for but not spotting the giant pimp's shiny head before finally taking another look over at my kneeling partner. Benny was busy on his cell phone, obviously calling in the EMT troops.

"That crazy dude's *bad*, man, no one to fuck wif," Double S continued when I glanced back down at him. "Big Leroy pushed The Prophet inna alley, then he growled, 'Fool, I gonna make sure ya'll 'member inna mornin' when ya look in the mirror, 'member *not* to ever mess again wif my bidness' then his hand was a blur, leavin' a black line from jus' under the outside corner of Prophet's lef' eye, 'cross his cheekbone to the corner of his mouf. Din't bleed fo' almost half a minute, ya know how a real sharp cut do. Then I see it open a bit and spot white cheekbone, jus' 'foh it gush red. Mean, nasty-ass cut. Ya unnerstan' what I'm sayin' here, Skip?"

"Yeah, you're saying Big Leroy purposely marked The Prophet for costing him business," I said, a little too loudly.

The legless man grimaced as if I'd struck him with my baton on one of his stumps. He glanced about anxiously to see if anyone had overheard me before nodding slightly, confirming my blurted accusation.

I slipped him a couple of bills. "Hey, thanks man, get yourself a snack and some joe up at All Star Donuts."

Short Stuff took the money, grinned, and scooted off up Leavenworth toward Post Street. Of course I knew he wasn't buying donuts or coffee with that bread. No, my man was dabbling with the glass pipe.

When I got closer to where Benny kneeled over The Prophet, I saw that my partner had given the injured man a clean handkerchief to staunch the flow of blood down his left cheek. The frail-looking old black man was propped up on a stack of cardboard, pressing the red-soaked hanky against his slashed face, deflecting the last of Benny's questions. Not looking too bad, really, all things considered.

He nodded at me as I kneeled.

"Yo, Skip," the old man said like a ventriloquist, trying not to move his mouth much.

I nodded back, smiling wryly.

We'd known each other for I guess about five years, ever since he'd shown up in the Tenderloin. Back then The Prophet wasn't a religious nut, just plain old Gent Brown.

"Got yourself in a little deep with Big Leroy?" I said, not really expecting him to acknowledge his attacker.

"Jus' preachin' the Word, Skip," he said with effort, chopping off the sentence as if he were short of breath, the hurt obvious in his dark eyes. "Bad times is comin', jus' 'round the corner for all the sinners here in the 'loin." He pressed on in spite of the pain. "The Man be comin' back. I see it clearer and clearer—"

I held up my hand as he warmed up, having heard his apocalyptic rant a number of times, including two weeks before, after a pair of teenage crack dealers had beaten the shit out of him with a piece of garden hose and a toy bat down on Taylor Street. He'd apparently broken up a sale with his spiel. "Okay, save your breath, and take it easy, Gent, the ambulance will be here any minute now." I patted his shoulder, lit up a Winston, and gave it to him, knowing the cigarette would keep him quiet for a moment or two, hoping the EMTs would hurry. Benny's handkerchief was sopping wet with blood, but Gent was not really in shock or anything—his eyes were clear, he was alert and coherent despite the deep cut. A tough old geezer, I thought, shaking my head with grudging admiration.

The EMTs showed up about a minute later, and I nodded goodbye as they loaded Gent into the ambulance. It wouldn't have done much good to press and get a statement from him because he wouldn't implicate Big Leroy. Preacher or no preacher, Gent Brown wasn't into suicide. Benny and I would just have to catch the giant on the street sometime and try to shake him up, which wasn't too likely; the mean-ass pimp was tougher than a piece of stale beef jerky .

Anyhow, the iceworm was resting, maybe even asleep. I felt pretty relaxed myself now that the 5150 was resolved. I absently watched the ambulance take off and the crowd disperse, thinking back on The Prophet's transformation.

I had first met Gent Brown when I'd responded to a shoplifting call up on O'Farrell near Van Ness about five years before. He was a common wethead back then, a Tenderloin stumblebum. He'd tried snagging a liter of red from the Korean's liquor store. Big_mistake. Mr. Pak had thrown down on Gent with a .44 Magnum cannon that he kept within reach under the checkout counter, stopping the old bum from leaving the store with the shoplifted bottle and keeping him frozen in place, staring at the open end of that handgun, as Mr. Pak called 911.

I didn't think too much about it at the time, just took Gent Brown outside for a get-yourself-cleaned-up lecture before I dropped him over at St. Anthony's for something to eat—an overcrowded jail wouldn't have helped him at all.

But the same kind of no-account life went on for Gent for the next four years, the old boy stumbling around the 'loin, panhandling, shoplifting, doing whatever it took to keep himself full of antifreeze. Feeling sorry for him, I slipped him an occasional buck or two at the end of the month when his social security was long gone. Then something odd happened to him one night, around midnight in an alley where he had his cardboard tent set up. The next day, he told me he'd had a vision, that he'd got "The Call" from a skinny-ass transvestite named Angel who had died a month previously of some infection complicated by her AIDS. Which I guess makes you kind of wonder about the Big Guy's recruitment staff.

Anyhow, whatever really happened, Gent cleaned up his act overnight. Got a room in the Reo residential hotel on Hyde, lived exclusively off his SSI, and quickly became one of the good guys around the 'loin. He volunteered at St. Anthony's handing out clean needles and condoms to junkies, helped homeless folks hook up with needed social services, and preached on the street. Soon after that, he became known around the 'loin as The Prophet.

But about six months ago his preaching turned to hardcore fundamental sermons, and lately they were laced with hard-edged fire and brimstone rants about the evils of the city, going off about all the sinners and the coming of the apocalypse. He turned from helping poor people to getting in their faces over their weaknesses and vices, becoming a major pain in the ass to a lot of folks down in the 'loin. Almost a low grade 5150, usually drawing an audience of little more than parking meters; folks scattered when they saw him coming.

This was all too much for me to worry about, because I had a six-pack of troubles of my own.

On the way to my apartment on O'Farrell, I picked up some taco chips, bean dip, a quart of vodka, and a twelve-pack of Bud: dinner. The bean dip was my concession to health food.

Inside the shabby digs, I flicked on the TV—Steve McQueen movie, one of my favorites, the Devil's Island one—and settled into my easy chair, popping a can of beer, relieved that the call hadn't turned shitty, not like that fiasco at the Bluenote four years ago last month.

Michael James, my long-time partner back then and a good man, had taken a .22 hollow point in the head after we'd rolled on the 5150 and walked into the open door of the seedy bar over on Jones. A homeboy, dusted-up good with PCP, had his piece out and capped Mike, who had strolled in a half-step ahead of me. At the sound of the gunshot, I had hit the deck and dug in, my equipment belt twisted around and my holstered piece trapped underneath me. I'd stared into Mike's frozen expression, shaking like a dog shitting peach pits. The bartender had finally slipped out from behind the bar and subdued the perp with a baseball bat to the back of his head.

For months after that night I'd had nightmares, seeing Mike's surprised face with that innocent tiny blue-ringed hole in his forehead oozing just a drop or two of blood, then waking up in a clammy sweat. After that, I got up close and personal with some serious boozing. I called in sick often or showed up for work hung over, and of course I drank on the job. Before that I had always been a decent blue, cited twice, a half-assed hero on one occasion when I had saved a toddler in a hostage situation. But that all changed when Mike bought it. After that night every 5150 froze my shit.

Then, a little over two years ago, the ballbuster.

We'd responded to a 5150 at a neighborhood market down on Hyde. My heart had been hammering, my pulse racing, my asshole puckered up, and my judgment messed up big time.

A Latino wearing a blue bandanna around his forehead bolted out the front door of the market just as we pulled up in front. My partner jumped out of the patrol car, weapon drawn, and shouted, "Halt! Halt! Halt!" He fired off a warning round into the air, following the book, SOP.

The guy pulled up to a stop after that, not quite a half a block away. He turned to face us, wearing that blue headband and a grey Pendleton shirt outside his baggy tan pants.

It turned surreal at that moment, everything moving in super slow motion, like I was detached from it all, watching an NFL replay on Sunday. My partner ordered the guy to raise his hands. Instead of obeying, he smiled goofy-like and reached inside his Pendleton near his belt. His hand came up and out, holding something dark—

And then he flew backward, looking startled as a big wet crimson stain spread across the front of his grey Pendleton. His knees gave way as the strength drained from his legs, and he collapsed.

I looked down in disbelief at the gun clutched in my sweaty hand. God Almighty!

In shock, I shuffled closer to the crumpled figure.

My partner bent over and lifted a black comb from the guy's hand.

Turned out the dead Latino was a twelve-year-old kid from the neighborhood. After sniffing glue with a pair of friends, he had entered the grocery and scared the owner with his erratic behavior. The frightened storekeeper had called 911. As we'd arrived, the boy had bolted out of the store right into us, confused, only reaching for his stupid-ass comb, apparently a nervous habit. All I had seen was a .38 Special.

Of course there was an IAD investigation and hearing, but I was cleared after two months. I took an additional two months off after that, not getting much from the visits with the head doctors. Just sat around home, often fighting with Diane, mostly getting well acquainted with various brands of cheap vodka and shaking hands with a steady supply of Bud tall boys. I checked out all the HBO and Showtime movies, seeing some of them two, three times in one day, remembering nothing. Eventually economics forced me back to work. I tried several times to transfer out of the Tenderloin. No luck. They stuck me with a series of rookie partners like Benny, who would move on soon; nobody wanted to partner up steady with me.

I got up from the chair, stumbled across the room, and flipped off the TV—McQueen was floating away to freedom on a raft. I really liked that final image. Half a dozen empty beer cans were sitting on the TV tray I used as an end table next to my Eazy Boy recliner. The chair had been the only piece of furniture I'd brought along when I left Diane and our Sunset place a couple months ago.

She'd come home last April with the bad results from Doctor Serra at Kaiser. They'd said colon cancer, inoperable, but of course I knew better. She had the iceworm, same as me; I must have infected her sometime before that doctor's visit.

So I left Diane, not wanting to watch her die. Or maybe just to get away from her nagging about my drinking. Who knows? My thinking was not too clear at that point. In any event, I'd moved into this studio dump on O'Farrell on the edge of the 'loin. Oddly, the medical experts at Kaiser could find nothing wrong with me even after several GI probes and X-rays with that barium crap. The fucking iceworm only burrowed deeper, able to hide from the doctors and the tests. Hibernated sometimes. For sure, the damn thing wasn't killing me fast like it was with Diane.

I sighed and shuffled into the tiny bathroom to take a piss, glancing at my mug in the mirror over the toilet. It said fifty-two on my California driver's license, but my reflection was a stranger, some beat-up old guy, at least sixty-five. "Man, hang on," I instructed the reflection. "Two more weeks, dude."

At that moment, the front door burst open, startling me.

A familiar voice said, "Hey, Skippy, you home?"

Nicki Machado, my roommate.

"Yeah, babe, in here taking a leak."

She peeked around the corner, trying to raise her eyebrows like Groucho Marx and leer lustfully at my johnson. She was a little worse for wear; her mascara was smudged, her lipstick not quite centered on her usually attractive full lips, and only one cheek had been rouged, making her look clownlike, silly not sexy.

She frowned uncharacteristically. "Couldn't find Smokey any-where again today," she said, referring to her kitten that had dis-appeared two nights ago. Of course I knew what had happened to the cat. In a drunken frenzy I'd tossed it down the old elevator shaft at the end of our hall, through the doors permanently stuck apart eighteen inches or so. The kitten hadn't made a peep, just a sickening, echoing wet *splat*. So I'd restacked the two big card-board boxes in front of the open shaft—management's idea of hi-tech security. The boxes may have been too heavy for a toddler to move, but were easily scooted clear by the three elementary school age Asian kids who sometimes played out in the hallway. So far the owners hadn't been cited for safety violations, or if so, management had ignored the citations.

Nicki had probably done most of her evening's searching down at The Greek's, the bar around the corner.

My roomie was in her late forties, a cop on disability for the last year or so—shot up in a botched liquor store robbery over in the Haight. Still had a trim, athletic body, except for her two extra belly buttons—the ugly red 9mm scars near her navel. She had dark, sexy good looks when she was sober and dressed nice, which wasn't too often anymore.

She spotted the groceries and vodka on the counter. "Hey, Skippy, fix you a drink?" she asked cheerily, sampling the taco chips and bean dip.

I nodded.

We each had a couple of generous hits from the bottle, and then Nicki got friendly. Kissing me. Exploring the inside of my mouth with her tongue. Placing her hands under my T-shirt, ca-ressing my chest and stomach, tentatively edging her hand inside my shorts. She broke off and whispered huskily, "You wanna do the short yo-yo tonight, Skippy?"

I nuzzled her neck. *Yeah, not a bad idea,* I thought. It had been quite a while since a one-on-one.

A few minutes later, the radio station K-FOG played backup to our rassling match. The two of us lay naked and sweaty on the bed, Nicki on top like she preferred, pinning my shoulders down with her hands. She moved her hips slowly in time to the Eagles' long instrumental introduction to "Hotel California," her eyes closed, her expression dreamy. As the song ended, Nicki bucked, shuddered, moaned, blinked, and smiled; then she kissed me sloppily on the lips.

"Skippy, you're a stud," she rasped. "You lay right there and I'll get you a drink."

It had indeed gone better than usual. Last couple of times, Nicki had been too dry, and by the time she'd returned from the bathroom with the KY gel, I had lost interest; too tired, or too old, or too limp, or just too fucked up from the booze to work up enthusiasm again. Often the iceworm was reawakened by all the sweaty activity, gnawing away like mad and ruining everything.

She got up, not trying to cover up her slight, girlish breasts with their huge, dark aureoles, the nipples still engorged and standing out almost half an inch, or even hiding her thick, unruly black pubic thatch, now damp. Unembarrassed. No false modesty with Nicki. Something else I kinda liked about her.

"Got a letter from Ray today," she said, her voice slightly slurred, smiling and handing me the drink of vodka—three fingers neat.

Ray was her son, a computer whiz working in North Carolina. He'd been concerned about her welfare after the shooting, wanting her to come out and stay with his family. But Nicki had resisted his calls and letters to date, telling me that Ray had a young wife and a two-year-old to care for. He didn't need a boozy old lady hanging around; besides, she was going back to work real soon, right after she got her act cleaned up.

She was probably right about the old lady part, but deep down we both knew she wasn't going back to police work ever again. It would've been so easy for her to give in, let her son take care of her, but she still had a little pride left—something else I envied. And she wasn't any trouble living with me in the tiny apartment, even with her kitten.

I felt a little surge of guilt well up into my consciousness over snuffing Smokey just because he'd been meowing loudly to get in at the same time the iceworm had reared up and gnawed away unmercifully, but I managed to force the feeling to the back of my mind: something I was getting pretty damned good at ever since going back to work after whacking the Latino kid.

I got up and joined her for another drink, both of us sitting around and chatting drunkenly in our birthday suits, not much giving a shit how we looked. A couple of worthless, broken-down old cops trying to provide some needed comfort to each other.

Late that same night, Nicki awakened me with a loud groan. She sat up next to me in bed, then doubled over in pain. Through clenched teeth, she described an icy gnawing sensation deep in her stomach. "Maybe scar tissue broken loose, Skippy," she whispered weakly, rubbing the two scars near her navel, her face contorted with pain. "Or even an ulcer. I been hitting the juice pretty hard ever since the shooting, you know."

I nodded, making no comment.

She described the sharp, biting pain in detail between gasps for breath.

I nodded, got up, and gave her the last of the vodka mixed with a little milk from the fridge. "Maybe this will help."

She grimaced, but managed to get the mix down. In a few minutes the pain lines in her face eased up. "I feel better. Thanks, Skippy." She smiled and kissed me gratefully on the lips.

I kissed her back, forcing a smile.

Of course it wasn't scar tissue or an ulcer that had awakened her in the middle of the night. No way. It was the fucking iceworm. I'd probably infected her by having unprotected sex, just like I'd done with Diane. What an asshole. I had to do something to help her, for Christ's sake.

But what could I do? I couldn't even drown the hidden devil in my own gut.

* * *

10:00 p.m. Friday night: one week from retirement, everything slow and easy in the Tenderloin. *Just hold on for another week,* I prayed as we patrolled along the upper fringe of the 'loin. We cruised along, relaxed-like, absently checking out the hookers, junkies, and dealers along the street. Nothing really unusual happened, nothing out of line.

Then we spotted Gent Brown signaling us over to the corner of O'Farrell and Hyde. Benny braked the car and double parked.

"Yo, Skip, got a minute, man?" The Prophet asked, gesturing for me to step out for a private moment.

I nodded, figuring he was ready to give up Big Leroy. Even though I was nervous anywhere near the Hyde Street store, I got out of the patrol car and moved closer to the old man. That's when I noticed his face looked funny, stitches out already, barely a scar noticeable on his cheek. Everything had healed up well; too well. Weird, because that had been a bone-deep razor cut only a week ago.

"What's up?" I asked, squinting and checking his healed wound a little closer. Yeah, just a slight red mark, little more than a shaving burn.

"It's you, man," Gent said, pointing an accusing finger at my chest. His tone wasn't sharp or strident as was usual when lecturing someone, but soft, gentle, like the expression on his face.

"Me?"

"Yeah, Skip, you gotta get your affairs in order, man. Time is runnin' out—"

"Hold off, Gent," I protested, bringing up both hands.

He just smiled, ignored my protest, and continued, "I'm serious, man, you only got a couple of days at most. You need to get rid of that ex-cop girlfriend. Your wife needs your support right now. You need to make amends, because the Grand Judgment Day beckons soon." At that point, he placed his hand on my shoulder in a fatherly gesture.

Whoa!

It felt like I had been touched with a live 440-volt wire. The electric shock traveled the length of my body and transported me to another place.

I was home, back in the Sunset, in our bedroom, looking down at Diane stretched out on our king-sized bed. She was pale and skinny, asleep but gasping for breath. A bright green kerchief partially covered her bald head.

The view shifted, and it was like time running backwards. I saw Diane and myself, both younger, in the backyard barbecuing with friends at my 40th birthday party; an even younger Diane in a new dress dancing at The Top of the Mark; earlier, in our first apartment in the Mission, making love, frantic and slippery, a couple of eager youngsters; our wedding day. All happy times in the distant past with hopes for the family that had never come.

I shuddered and moaned, breaking the man's electric grip on my shoulder. The vision disappeared.

Gent nodded, as if privy to all I had seen. "Hurry, make peace with her now, or you will be sorry on Judgment Day. Time to act is short. Give up the juice. Go home for good, Skip, leave the 'loin behind *now*." His tone had taken on a sharper edge, moving up in pitch. His eyes were clear and shining brightly.

I pulled away from him, feeling weak-kneed, stunned by the shock to my system and especially the vivid vision or hallucination or whatever the fuck it was. Sweating, I nodded as if agreeing with The Prophet but quickly retreated back into the patrol car.

"Let's get out of here," I whispered out of the side of my mouth to my partner. "Now, man, now!"

Benny dropped the car into gear and drove off. Glancing over at me, he asked, "What happened back there, Skip? You look like you've seen a ghost."

"Maybe I did, at that," I answered weakly, remembering how bad Diane had looked. Automatically, I reached under the seat for my Crystal Geyser bottle. The iceworm was awake and beginning to feed.

Saturday night I awakened in a cold sweat.

"What's the matter, honey?" Nicki asked sleepily, glancing at the bedside digital clock: 2:37 a.m.

"Nothing, babe, just a bad dream. Go back to sleep," I said dismissively, but I was shaken because I had experienced the first part of the vision again, updated: Diane obviously dying, looking even worse than the first vision when The Prophet had grabbed my shoulder; her older sister at her bedside.

I got up, went out to the kitchen and drained a Bud, idly glancing out the window at the signboard on the roof of the building across the way. A blue neon message flashed in the foggy night: NOW, SKIP! NOW, SKIP! NOW, SKIP!

I blinked and the signboard was dark as usual at this hour.

Holy shit!

The booze had finally gotten to me.

I was going around the corner big time, hallucinating, and Gent Brown had packed my bags.

I paced about for a few minutes, finally focusing on the real cause of all my trouble.

It wasn't Gent or even the booze.

No, not really; it was the fucking iceworm.

I had to do something about it for the sake of all three of us—Diane was dying, Nicki was hurting, and I was being driven crazy by the damned thing. Standing there in the dark at 3:00 a.m., I knew what I had to do. *Okay*, I thought, smoothing it all out in my mind, dividing it into three steps.

A few minutes later, with no one up yet in the building, I dressed. I slid my Glock 9mm into my belt in the hollow of my back, concealed under my T-shirt, and took a long, deep breath. Finally, I awakened Nicki.

"Babe, get up. I heard Smokey crying. I think I know where he is."

"Wha—? Smokey?"

She struggled up, confused, but finally grasped my meaning.

"Yes, now slip on your stuff."

Nicki pulled on her jeans and a T-shirt, running her hands through her hair. Then she looked at me expectantly, her expression still dazed. "Where is he?"

"C'mon," I said, beckoning her follow me out into the hallway.

The building was graveyard quiet.

"This way."

I led her down the hall to the old elevator shaft. As hoped, she meekly followed me, not asking questions, still half asleep and anxious about the welfare of her kitten. At the shaft, I pushed aside the boxes, exposing the gap in the elevator doors. "He fell down there," I said, pointing down into the blackness, the smell of something rotten almost making me gag.

"Smokey? Smokey, baby, you down there?" Nicki said, kneeling and leaning forward into the shaft.

I blinked, my eyes tearing up, my hands shaking as if I had Parkinson's. *Do it now, man,* I told myself.

But I hesitated drawing my gun, thinking it would be easier to just give her a quick nudge...but she might survive the fall; then what?

Nicki glanced back at me. "God, what is that smell?" she said, rubbing her nose. She peered back down the darkened shaft. "You sure Smokey is down there?" she asked, her voice tight, mixed with hope and dread. "Smokey?"

"Yeah," I replied, resigned to the original plan. I pulled the automatic out from under my shirt, my hand trembling. I eased the weapon up, sucking in a deep breath. "He's down there, babe, I promise." Then, through my blurred gaze, I picked a spot just behind her left ear, steadied myself, and squeezed the trigger. The shot echoed loudly down the elevator shaft.

Instantly, Nicki tumbled forward, disappearing into the darkness.

Splat, then silence.

"He's there, babe," I said, my voice a barely audible, scratchy whisper. "You found your Smokey." I wiped my eyes and runny nose on a hanky before tossing it down after Nicki, then added, "And the fucking iceworm ain't going to hurt you no more either."

I turned away, fighting back the tears, and hurried down the hallway to the stairwell as I heard people in the apartments beginning to stir, awakened by the echoing gunshot.

A little later, still very early in the morning, I found the extra key on the nail partially driven into the back porch overhang, where it was always kept at our place in Sunset. After letting myself in quietly, I tiptoed down to the spare bedroom. Everything happened in slow motion as if I were watching some dark movie with time geared down. Diane's older sister, Robin, was asleep and snoring loudly. She was a physician's assistant, recently retired from the ER at UCSF. As I thought, she'd moved in and been taking care of Diane, at least the last week or so.

I tiptoed down the hall to the master bedroom.

Diane was asleep. Hospital-room bottles hung on supports on either side of the bed, one probably morphine, the medicine dripping down lines into shunts taped on the backs of both her hands. Her breathing was labored but steady, her lips chapped and flakey, her face emaciated and chalky pale. So skinny under her nightshirt.

The iceworm was eating her alive.

"I'm sorry, ba—" I whispered, a huge lump rising in my throat, choking off the rest of my apology.

Well, I will take care of everything now, I thought, sucking in a deep breath, resigned to completing the second part of my plan.

Choked up, teary-eyed, but able to move on automatic pilot, I bent over the frail woman I had once loved dearly, and I pressed a pillow over her face.

She struggled frantically, but I pushed down with all my weight. Her feet made a few weak cycling movements, kicking off the sheet...then nothing. Diane was gone. She wasn't going to suffer anymore.

I tiptoed back down the hall, past my sleeping sister-in-law, and then let myself quietly out of the house while the neighborhood still slept in the early morning fog.

Back in the apartment in the 'loin, I sat sipping a Bud, thinking about the plan in the pre-dawn darkness.

I felt better about doing something good for a change, helping both Nicki and Diane, their iceworms stilled. I sighed and looked down at the table, the Glock wiped clean and just sitting there waiting next to my beer. I picked up the can and drained the Bud. Surprisingly, my devil had been quiet all morning, ever since

Nicki had tumbled down the elevator shaft.

"Uh-huh, running a low profile, you shitty bastard," I said aloud, grinning wryly to myself. "Well, it's too fucking late, boyo!" I picked up my gun, jacking a round into the chamber. Time to take care of step three.

But I faltered, an intense wave of fear washing over me, speeding my heart rate and pulse. My eyelid twitched out of control; my hands grew slippery and shook badly.

"You can do it, man," I whispered unconvincingly, my grip on the Glock baby weak.

That's when I heard it. A faint scratching sound at the hallway door.

Then a familiar mewling.

"No way," I whispered, shaking my head in denial but lacking any real conviction.

I stood up, slipping the gun into my belt, and crossed the room, nervously easing open the front door.

Smokey, tail standing up, walked in and brushed himself against my right ankle. He looked exactly the same; maybe a little scuffed up and dirty, but unhurt.

Shocked, I remained in place for a few moments, rubbing my eyes. The kitten purred around my ankle. What the fuck was going on? An icicle stabbed into my gut, the iceworm waking in a frenzy. Momentarily ignoring the pain, I leaned out into the hallway, peering left down toward the shaft, half expecting to see Nicki.

Nothing.

But the cat was there, no question about that.

Suddenly, it took off running, back out the door and into the hallway.

"Wait, Smokey!" I shouted, following the grey kitten down the stairwell.

Out on the street, I pulled up short, stunned and gasping for breath.

The whole frigging Tenderloin appeared to be on fire from where I stood, smoke and flames leaping up from the nearby buildings into the darkness.

Sirens wailed in the distance. A fire truck appeared, sliding around the corner, and then pulling up in front of my building, spilling out its crew. They pulled off their fire hoses and hooked up to the nearby water hydrants.

A screaming patrol car braked just up the street.

Looking that direction, past the firemen and cops, I spotted Smokey among the crowd. Folks from nearby apartments milled in the street, many only half-dressed, peering around wide-eyed at the inferno raging around them.

On some silent cue, everyone began to move *en masse* downtown.

I followed the crowd for several blocks. At the corner of O'Farrell and Market Street I paused, looked both ways, and watched what looked like all of downtown San Francisco spilling out from the nearby streets that fed into Market—hundreds, perhaps thousands, of people.

What is going on?

9/11 flashed into my head.

Another terrorist attack? Maybe one of those suitcase nuclear devices going off around in a building, setting everything afire, people lit up with radiation?

I noticed that some of the crowd did look kind of funny, not glowing with radiation, but wearing peculiar, stunned expressions, their clothes dirty and scuffed up. They shuffled along as if they'd stepped out of one of those George Romero movies.

At that moment the ground bucked and the street in front of me cracked open with a loud snapping *pop*. The sidewalk rolled as if it had turned to Jell-O, knocking people to their knees.

I grabbed the closest parking meter and hung on, looking up in awe as streaks of jagged lightning ripped across the sky. Lower, just above the building tops, neon blue balls of psychedelic fire were tumbling over and over, rolling westerly in the direction of Civic Center. Accompanying the spectacular light show was an orchestra of chaos: thunder, boulders crashing into nearby canyons, more sirens wailing from every direction, sporadic explosions in buildings. Debris tore away overhead and crashed down onto the street. Cars braked and collided; frightened people shouted and cried. Some were struck down by falling objects and screamed out in pain.

Still clutching the parking meter as an anchor, I looked around at ground level, trying to take it all in.

That's when I spotted *them*, down by the Ferry Building: black-cloaked horsemen astride ebony steeds thundering up Market Street, the magnificent beasts' eyes crimson, nostrils flaring and snorting fire, the riders scattering the crowd as they galloped by, four abreast, toward Civic Center.

"Yo, Skip."

Stunned by the whole phantasmagoric scene, I finally dropped my gaze, looking down at the foot of the parking meter.

It was Short Stuff.

I couldn't speak for a moment, but eventually managed a raspy whisper, "What's happening here, Double S?"

He wasn't wearing his normal laid-back, half-assed cynical expression. Instead, he looked kind of whacked-out, awestruck himself. Still, he spoke calmly in spite of all that was happening around us. "Hey, this gotta be the shitstorm The Prophet been rantin' 'bout."

"Shitstorm?" I repeated as fragments of building material crashed just a few yards away from where we stood, flattening a Volvo station wagon parked on the street and covering us with a thin layer of dust.

"Yeah, ya know, that pocket-leaps jive he been preachin' 'bout," the crippled man said, wiping his dirty face on his sweatshirt sleeve. "Dead raisin' up...that's them muthahfuckahs out there, ya know, the stupid-lookin', scuffed-up ones, shufflin' along like a chain gang."

I looked where he pointed, out into the crowd. Every other person indeed looked stoned, marching along in lockstep, zombie-like. But arisen from the dead?

"Oh yeah, Skip, the shit done hit the fan, big time, ya unnerstan' what I'm sayin'?" Double S continued over the hubbub, snorting and spitting mud out into the gutter. "Uh-huh, and check *him* out, now. Guess he ain't jus a prophet no mo'. Uh-uh, he gotta be Da Man!"

I glanced in the direction of his gesture; the crowd was gathering back in the street after the horsemen galloped by, coalescing tightly around a nearby figure.

Gent Brown.

All dressed up in a flowing golden robe, so bright it made me squint. He sure didn't resemble any Tenderloin wethead or stumblebum now, nor any street preacher either. No way. He drifted up Market Street, gathering people behind him. The crowd moved in the general direction of Civic Center.

Holy shit!

Close behind Gent, in the middle of the crowd, was Nicki, wearing a dazed expression, shuffling along in step with the others. "Hey, babe!" I shouted and waved uselessly as she disappeared from view, lost in the hubbub.

"C'mon, Skip, guess we bettah fall in our ownselves. Maybe get the word at Civic Center, ya hear me?" Double S pushed off on his scooterboard, not waiting for my response.

At that moment the iceworm reared up, thrashing about in a frenzy, doubling me over. I grabbed my stomach, the pain incredible, and looked down, half expecting to see the devil explode out of my body like that gut-wrenching scene in the movie *Alien.*

God Almighty!

I had indeed gone around the corner, for sure. The iceworm had driven me crazier than a shithouse mouse. This must be some kind of crazy-ass shit, an elaborate, grand delusion. No, I wasn't following any hallucination to Civic Center or anywhere else. And even if they were real, I was going to do what was right. Finish what I'd started with Diane and Nicki. Take care of the iceworm *now*, once and for all, and worry about salvation and resurrection later.

Sweat soaking my shirt, vision tunneling, and my right eyelid going bananas, I choked up. I was in bad shape.

The revelation hit me hard: *I could not do it.* No way.

As I had suspected earlier, before Smokey's scratching had distracted me, I just did not have the stones to go out the traditional cop way. The admission brought tears to my eyes.

"You lousy, fucking pussy—"

Wait.

Maybe, just maybe, I could still go out stand-up. A good chance *if* all this was bogus, just happening in my head.

With heavy legs, I stumbled past the debris on the sidewalk to a corner phone kiosk and dug two quarters from my pocket, hoping the damn thing still worked. Amazing: a dial tone.

I called dispatch at the station, and, surprisingly, someone picked the phone up on the first ring. After identifying myself and giving my badge number, I laid it on them, the whole maryann.

"...That's right, a total 5150 going fucking ballistic on lower Market...I'm at the corner of O'Farrell...Yeah, armed," I finished in an exhausted voice, letting the phone slip out of my trembling left hand. I slumped down on my butt, back against the phone stand, and waited, the Glock resting in my lap. Something crashed nearby behind me, covering me with a thick coating of dust.

I didn't turn, just squeezed my eyes shut against the pain in my gut and took several long, deep breaths. I concentrated on the white circle, blotting out everything around me.

Quiet now, real quiet.

Shitstorm gone.

Iceworm still.

AFTERWORD

Seven or eight years ago, I'd completed maybe two of these Tenderloin tales. Steve Savile, an underrated Brit writer and one time publisher of the press, Imaginary Worlds, had read both stories. He suggested that I write more Tenderloin stories and call the collection: *A Taste of Tenderloin*. Shortly after that Gord Rollo, the editor for *Unnatural Selection*, a fine anthology that sank almost unread by very many readers also thought it was a pretty good idea. Over the past five years I have concentrated mostly on novellas or novels, but occasionally finishing a short story. Each year or so I'd write another Tenderloin story. Last year I realized I had stories about quite a few different 'Loin residents, and enough tales for a good collection. Jason Sizemore of Apex Books agreed. So you have in hand the results of an eight-year process.

Thank you Steve for the idea, and Gord for the encouragement.

A paragraph about each story might be informative and of reader interest:

"Lost Patrol" is the most recently written tale but the events stretch back farthest in time to the early 60s. In my experience, when folks first come under hostile fire in the military they immediately become superstitious, reaching out for almost any good luck charm or soon developing beliefs in incredulous things. That's the case with the Lost Patrol, a legend from Vietnam. I think I still believe that platoon is still wandering around the jungle over there.

"Magic Words" was written for the publication *Dark Wisdom*, a slick magazine with colored illustrations for each tale. It also was written as a kind of counterpoint to my story "Magic Numbers," which appeared in *Borderlands 5*, a Stoker anthology winner. Both tales begin and end in alleys. Maybe I'll write another story some day and call it "Magic Colors," or some such, which of course will have to also end in an alley. Hmm....

"Tombstones in His Eyes" is full of well-researched drug lore that eventually has a place in several of my novels. Heroin is a big time problem in our country, no more so than in San Francisco, which authorities estimate has at least 12,500 addicts. A favorite charity of mine is the non-profit Walden House which does good work in San Francisco and throughout the California prison system in the area of drug rehab. The title of the story comes from street advice: How do I find a connection? Look for the guy with tombstones in his eyes.

"Bushido" incorporates some of my interest and admiration for the old Samurai culture of Japan. The epigram comes from a favorite film of mine, *The Last Samurai*. The Tenderloin is packed with shy, withdrawn people like the Ugly Man in the story. Perhaps many of them requiring mental health outreach services. What has been done recently is to gate many of the 'Loin's alleys so the homeless can't erect their cardboard tents. I wonder if that does much for their mental problems?

"Balance" is one of my favorite stories, and a 2006 Stoker finalist. Back in the 60s when disabled vets were beginning to return home from Vietnam, requiring medical services, I was aware of the deplorable condition of many VA hospitals, especially those in non-urban areas. As we have found out about even the highly visible Walter Reed Hospital, until recently conditions haven't changed much. I also couldn't resist the dramatic irony of an ex-Force Recon Marine running his own special operation in the 'Loin. His particular delusion actual came from a real case of a serial murderer who believed in something like the Law of Catastrophic Geo-Homeostatis (my title). He moves back and forth from Vacaville Correctional Medical Facility to San Quentin, depending on his current mental evaluation by the State.

"The Apotheosis of Nathan McKee" first appeared in Gord Rollo's anthology, *Unnatural Selection*. Gord wanted me to do an invisible man and monster story. I said sure but gave it my own spin—no real monster. Recently I finished a novel, *Not Fade Away* which is based on this short story—actually an extension.

"Bruised Soul," is another of my favorites. A boxer returning from a State Hospital to the 'Loin. He had no where else to go. As some folks know I did a little boxing in my youth. The ex-boxer in this story may be more typical than folks imagine. I think there are many people in the Tenderloin like this character whose feet seem to be stuck in hardening cement. They just can't get out. The sad thing is that many of them know it. For those who would like to know more about the non-spectacular side of boxing, *Fat City* is a very realistic book . Or wait for my *Not Fade Away*. I think I do a pretty good job of explaining the attraction to the sport.

"5150" is probably a pretty realistic slice of an old cop's life in the City. Or anyone else who has just faded away in their job, hanging on until they can retire. I think the relationship between the cop and his girlfriend is both sad and touching. In this aspect of the story I suspect that what these two deal with isn't much different that what we all deal with in dysfunctional relationships.

AUTHOR BIO

Gene O'Neill lives in the Napa Valley with his wife, Kay, a primary grade teacher at St. Helena Elementary School. They have been married for 44 years; their grown children, Gavin and Kay Dee, live in Oakland and San Diego.

Gene has two degrees, neither having anything to do with writing (or much of anything else). At one time or another he has been a Marine, carried mail, worked on seismic crews exploring for oil, been a Right-of-Way Agent (appraised, acquired, condemned, and managed real property to build the interstate highway system around Sacramento), been a contract specialist for AAFES (contracting to bring private services like barbers, cleaners, and beauty parlors onto military bases), and vice president of a manufacturing plant. Gene describes his employment background as "rich, varied, and colorful." His brother-in-law, the president of the above plant, describes Gene as more of a "disgruntled ne'er-do-well."

Since surviving the Clarion Writers' Workshop in 1979, Gene has seen over 100 of his stories published, perhaps most notably: two in the Twilight Zone Magazine, six in the Magazine of Fantasy & Science Fiction, two in Pulpsmith, four in Science Fiction Age, three in Cemetery Dance, and several in various anthologies. Many of his past stories have garnered Nebula and Stoker recommendations, including "Balance," a Stoker finalist in 2007.

Gene writes full time now, recently putting the finishing touches on a novel, *Not Fade Away*. His novels *Lost Tribe*, *Shadow of the Dark Angel* and *Deathflash* are forthcoming in 2009/2010 from Bad Moon Books.

ARTIST BIO

In 1962 in the bucolic region of Southern Indiana, a peculiar child was born and given the name of **Steven Charles Gilberts**. Being the only Indiana bred person in a family of Wisconsin origin, this led to the unfortunate child being labeled "hoosier" by his extended family; a group collectively known as "badgers," "cheese heads," and perhaps most frightening of all, Norwegians.

Steven and his lovely wife Becky now live in a spooky Queen Ann cottage within a small Dunwich-esk village of southern Indiana, near the now abandoned ammo plant of his youth. While hiding from the townsfolk, Steven concocts odd illustrations for the small press industry.

INTRODUCTION BIO

Gavin O'Neill has covered lots of weird action for the *San Francisco Bay Guardian*, and published dark fiction and poetry in respected literary journals. He holds an MFA from the University of Oregon where he taught fiction writing. He is the unfortunate son of horror writer Gene O'Neill.

The Bram Stoker Award-nominated novella "Mama's Boy" is the cornerstone of this 14-story collection from author, Fran Friel, and Apex Publications. Packed with 280 pages of demented, post-traumatic, brutally chilling horror, these stories will linger. They will haunt. They will accompany you into the night.

ISBN TB: 978-0981639086
ISBN HB: 978-0-9816390-7-9
www.apexbookcompany.com

Breinigsville, PA USA
10 November 2009
227359BV00001B/4/P